Weathernose by Maram Taibah

ISBN: 978-1-7333620-0-9

To Yuyu.

FORWARD

Tart appeared to me one summer afternoon, standing on the shore of his Island. Cypress did not come until later and she was a fresh surprise to me as I hope she was to you. I spent my college years dabbling with this story and other narratives for this pair as well. And then I buried them because I wasn't ready to share them with the world. But, still, I dreamed of the day when I would finally settle down and write more Tart and Cypress stories.

So here you go. I'm sharing this little book with you. I hope you hate-love Cypress as much as I do. I hope you're not very much like Tart because then you'd be lonely. And if you are, I feel you.

Thank you for picking up this book.

CHAPTER ONE

I N THE SIDEWAYS HEMISPHERE of the Cerulean Universe, there was a roaming archipelago that went, for the most part, unnoticed by anybody. If you looked at it from above, you would see one tiny island existing on its own, like a freckle, not too far from the city of Linett. On this island, there lived a weatherman.

His name was Tart. When he was born, there were many offended whispers from the elderly folk in his family. But he never wondered about his name. It had always been there, just like his hands and feet, though at the wise age of ten he decided it was ridiculous to be named after a dessert. The name stayed because it suited him as he grew into it.

At the age of forty-two he had long ago lost his boyish roundness, and the disparity between his looks and his name became all the more noticeable. He now had a lean, taut build, interrupted by aged skin at the creases. His hair was a mouse brown carpet that seemed to ripple up in spikes whenever he was annoyed. It was said that he had inherited the abnormal sharpness of his nose from a long-forgotten great uncle. Coming from a family that produced a consistent type of offspring, his strange nose had always offended his mother, who thought it looked like the tusk of an Arctic narwhal.

Tart was the only weatherman in Linett, and the People's Meteorology Organization (PMO) paid him *very* well. His days were made up of wind, rain, and air pressure. All he had to do in a day's work was to produce the measurements. The promise of sameness made it a comfortable thing to get out of bed every morning, and to his mind there was no reason that today should be any different. But days, as we all know, can be deceiving.

He woke up at eight o'clock. His morning routine got him out of bed, into the shower, and upon a moldy piece of toast. He bustled around in his orderly mess for a cup of coffee and a slice of butter. He stopped in the middle of it to be surprised at a thought: the foot of his bed was almost nose-to-nose with his kitchen table. He could have had a wall built there, but what did it matter that he slept where he ate?

His routine then took him to his workshop, where he recalculated last night's work. Tomorrow's weather forecast was ready. He rolled up the sheaf of paper on which was printed a neat assembly of symbols for the conditions of the sky. Clear. Sunny—as always this time of year. Humidity at forty-three percent. Sunrise. Sunset. It was a study of tomorrow, a calculation of the elements, not of the happiness or misery that it would bring to anybody.

On his island, Tart had the luxury not to worry about a thing. There was no one and nothing there but him, his pet crow Kra, his bleached hut, and his workshop. Being close to the elements kept him content here. The rolling fabric of sand along the beach, the endless azure straight on and around, uninterrupted by other inhabited lands. The thick trees by the beach trapped the moisture and wove a verdant net against the sky. He was content to walk barefoot, sometimes with no shirt on. Day and night, he heard nothing but the sound of the sea's breathing and his own.

Today, he noticed a vague uneasiness on his skin, about his shoulders, that he could not quite understand. He looked out the window. The sun glared fiercely. The sky was a boastful blue. The breeze was the kind you would want on your face as you read a book at the beach. But still.

He decided to do some more calculations. The barometer was a fiend this morning. He almost spilled his coffee into the tank of moisture balls. And there it was! A knot in the equations that he had failed to see. He started all over again. It was almost noon and the forecast was due. He took out a fresh form from the pile and began writing again. This time, as it turned out, it was not to be sunny at all tomorrow. In fact, there was a thunderstorm brewing. It was a wonder what a difference a single number made. But there you were! That was the source of the uneasiness, he convinced himself. There was nothing to worry about.

When he went outside to the beach, the forecast skipped from his hand into an unfurling breeze. Kra swooped down and caught it with his beak.

"Good catch," Tart mumbled. Kra nipped his neck.

But the portal was nowhere to be seen. The shaft through which he sent his daily report was sunken beneath the water. It was flat and level with the seabed. This had never happened before and it was a little insulting, the idea that the weather department failed to appreciate the hard work he put into his forecasts enough to ensure that no such silly errors occurred. *Lazy chap in the control room must have fallen asleep with his elbow on the retract button,* Tart thought. *They ought to pour coffee into his ears.* As though that settled it, he crouched down and looked at the round metal portal flickering underneath the waves. In normal circumstances the round shaft would be jutting out of the water. When the portal sensed motion, it opened and operated a vacuum, which then sent the forecast to the department via a pipe that stretched for miles, right into the mailroom. They had obliged him by building this method of communication so that he would not have to live on the mainland—with people.

But what to do about the portal today? The whole point of the pipe being above sea level was to keep the forecast from getting wet. Unless they invented waterproof paper in the next hour, there was no way to send the forecast. He put his hand in the water, feeling for the portal's embossed surface. It was just as he expected. The portal would obviously not open underwater. Wouldn't want to flood the system, now, would he?

Tart looked at Kra, who sat observantly on his shoulder, and pulled down his floppy straw hat in annoyance. He hurried off to the pier where his mossy ferry was bobbing.

As he walked up the plank, he felt it in an instant: a small, unrepressed shiver. He turned to look toward the southern sky. The air had lifted very slightly. An onslaught of clouds was traveling fast and near. It was one of the few times that he doubted his forecast. The storm was coming too soon.

He jumped on deck and started the clunky motor. A wheel of pedals turned, regurgitating water until the ferry set out into the butter-smooth sea.

At the helm he had a firm grip on the steering wheel. "If only this thing would up and fly!" he said, wincing at the painstaking pace.

The clouds in the south turned a nasty sheen of grey. Kra flew overhead.

"Any more of them, old boy?"

When the distance was more than half conquered, Tart leaned against the railings outside, having set the wheel for a steady, straight course. Linett was only twenty minutes away.

The green humps of the main island trickled at the far horizon. Linett looked very quiet and serene from this distance, almost like a shrine of worship, but once the ferry docked, all noise would be set loose like a rusty orchestra that would never stop.

CHAPTER TWO

O N THE PIER, TART braced himself. He felt the usual quiet in his head ebbing and giving way to abusive chaos. Even his shoes were beginning to make *shfft-shfft* sounds against the cobblestone that wound a path through the fisheries and caravans of sea-born trinkets.

He passed a fleet of rowboats that the little boys were in the habit of tying to the bobbing piers along the beach. The urchins were knee-deep in water with their muslin shalwars rolled up. Sunburned lads splashed sunburned girls who flocked together to ward them off.

Tart greeted this world with a grumpy grunt. His ears tuned very slowly into the hubbub of the city. There were laughs, rising babble, horses' whinnies, things being hefted, things being dropped, and the sudden pounding of the city's central clock announcing midday. The cobblestone eventually led into a wide, red dirt road where the crowd rushed. He had to apologize quite a few times after he'd bumped into people, not yet used to the feel of so many of them around. It was normal to bump into things here, but a thin uneasiness prickled on his skin. He felt as though he came from an entirely different race.

A young man wearing a turban slapped him with a fish.

"Watch it, you!" Tart cried.

It was then that he realized that a fish market had somehow materialized, and the reek of it that was forced into his nostrils was acutely offending.

It took him a few tries to find his way into a part of the city that practiced a little more decorum, but it was still a bother to be rid of the slippery stench of fish skins.

Tart decided to take the quieter lanes and alleyways to the weather department, away from the main roads. It was the longer path but the more alluring at the moment. The sheer madness of that pier and the sheer number of people! It was like the Day of Judgment, only everyone was happy.

He wound his way through many whitewashed houses. He passed through pleasantly aired sheets of laundry. He could smell shellfish being cooked in gargantuan pots of red broth. Children played hopping games and troubadours tuned their mandolins. Everyone seemed to be doing something, but it was a wonder to Tart how none of it seemed to be important or urgent.

The weather department, an offshoot of the meteorology complex, was half a mile into the city. The building's long rectangular shape created a pleasing crosshatch behind a row of tapering cypress trees.

Once inside, Tart rooted himself in the cool dark reception area of the main building to bask in the silence. At first glance—or first sniff—Tart sensed something strange. There was a smell. That was certain. It was not a perfume or a strong odor. It was closer to a scent that lingered upon the air, accessible only at every other breath. He sniffed some more. He was confronted now, not with the source of the smell, but with a painting above the reception desk. He stared at it with a creeping sense of apprehension. It was the same thickset gilded frame hung at the same slightly crooked angle. Only the picture was no longer of the smug founder of the weather department. Now it was a smartly painted portrait of a white rabbit.

And there was more. There were scribbles and sketches of strange gadgets, framed and hung in various nooks and panels. There was no longer a sign on his boss's door, which ought to have been the first true sign of impending chaos.

He knocked once. He knocked twice but didn't bother a third time. He pushed the door open and entered. The office was such a mess that it could have been a game of hidden objects. There was parchment, rolled and unrolled, strewn all over the floorboards. Some of his boss's ornaments were tipped over. The porcelain frog that Tart had never cared for had lost a nose and in its place had acquired a gaping black hole into the baked creature's insides. There was a havoc of things on top of the desk that had nothing to do with the weather department's business: clothes, hats, spectacles of many colors, a sleeping bird inside a small round cage and—a pair of briefs, which were flattened underneath the corner of a sprawling suitcase. Tart heard something crunch underneath his foot as he took a step forward into the scene. It was a turquoise peppermint that must have been kicked astray from a trail of peppermints by the foot of the desk.

Tart heard someone scuttling in the back room just off the wall to his left.

"Mr. Clockquirk!" Tart called.

The scuttling stopped. There was no answer.

"Mr. Clockquirk!"

"Er—yes! Who is it?"

Tart rolled his eyes. "It's Tart."

He heard a deep sigh coming through the wall.

"I heard that," Tart mumbled resentfully.

Finally, Mr. Clockquirk poked his oval head through the doorway. It was as though a shiny reddish potato with flyaway grey hair had grown through the wall. Precisely in the center of it, there was a big bee-stung nose.

"I'll be right there!" Mr. Clockquirk panted.

He came out carrying things which he must not have selected carefully upon entering. He stopped in his tracks and looked down at the teddy bear in his arms. He stuffed its head in the crook of his elbow and pretended, for the comfort of both men, that Tart had not seen it. All these things went into the gaping suitcase, which Clockquirk threw shut.

Any other person than Tart would cheerfully have asked, "Going somewhere?" but Tart stuffed his hands into his pockets, looking sour.

"My pipe is blocked."

"Well, of course it is."

"What?"

Mr. Clockquirk bent to pick up the peppermints.

"How am I supposed to send my forecast?" Tart asked. "If you want it that is!"

"We don't."

Perhaps Tart had not heard properly as Mr. Clockquirk was bent over and had just popped the last of the peppermints into his mouth. The light from the window dissolved into shadow all of a sudden. The storm arrived in Linett.

"I'm sorry. I didn't get that." Tart said.

Mr. Clockquirk dropped into his swivel chair.

"Tart, sit down."

Tart sat.

"I know the news must have been hard on you," Mr. Clockquirk said.

"What news?"

"But we really can't afford it any longer with the new developments."

"*What news?*"

"Don't pretend you don't know. I sent you a letter!"

"No, you didn't!"

Clockquirk got up again to throw the entire mess on the desk into the suitcase.

"I did. I sent it yesterday morning," Mr. Clockquirk said. "I have faith yet in our postal service you know!"

"What's happened?" Tart asked.

Mr. Clockquirk heaved the suitcase off the desk and onto the floor. Where the suitcase had been, a pile of rubbish appeared, among which was a formal envelope addressed to Tart.

Mr. Clockquirk gave a soft "Oh." He scratched his head. "Oh dear."

He seemed to take in his own state of disorderliness as he would a train that he had missed.

"Well this is yours." He offered it to Tart in exasperation.

With that, he lifted his bulging suitcase and did his best to get around Tart and be on his way.

"Where are you going?" Tart spluttered.

"I, my dear fellow, am going on vacation!"

He said it like he was fencing—with no one in particular, with the air, or with life itself.

"I wish you well in all of your endeavors, Tart!" he said. "*Goodbye!*"

"You're mad!" Tart called after him. "Does PMO know about this?"

Mr. Clockquirk was out the door. "Read the letter, Tart!"

But then he filled up the doorway again with his suitcase, his overcoat, and his bulbous nose. "And don't you *dare* accuse me of redecorating this place!"

CHAPTER THREE

My dear Tart,

There has been a significant change in the weather department. Living on that island of yours, you might not have heard of the new development, the new invention, which has caused quite a bit of riot all over Linett. News of it will probably reach the capital very soon.

The admirable Miss Cypress Korkul has invented the weathernose, which is a gadget that seems to do everything that you spend a whole day doing in one minute. What's more, the weathernose gives us the weather forecasts of two months and the highlights of a year.

My intention is not to enlighten you about this new technology, but rather to inform you that your services will not be needed from this day forward. I am sure that Miss Cypress's invention will soon become a worldwide phenomenon.

Therefore, I release you from your post at the weather department as daily forecaster.

If you wish to obtain more information, please contact Miss Korkul, who will, by the way, take my place as chief of the department while I am away on vacation for the entirety of the next year. You will find her very capable and delightful to talk to.

G. Clockquirk

Chief of Weather Department
The People's Meteorology Organization

It started to rain just then. The sound of a thousand little drums carried through the wooden beams across the ceiling. Tart stared between the dots of rain outside the window.

Cypress Korkul. The name just sat there and stared back. For now, it was attached to no form. All that he knew was that it was female. And there was a weathernose that came along with it.

Tart went outside. By the time he was on the pier, he was soaked. But the rain had stopped and the wind had lifted. The storm only licked at first before it battered. The weathernose must have known that.

He and Kra headed home. Sure enough, as Tart made himself a warm mug of milk and honey, the storm slapped his roof. It kept him indoors like a berated child who was forced to contemplate his misdeeds, or in this case, his future.

Cypress Korkul was real. He knew that. And she had outsmarted him. She took from him the one thing he had been doing, and proudly, for almost nineteen years. He thought about the machinery of life. It was strange how one went to sleep never suspecting that some great and life-altering thing would happen on the doorstep of the new day.

His day had always been as such: he would wake up before the sun. He would walk the shore of the entire island to invigorate his mind. At sunup he would greet Kra in his hut and they would share a breakfast, through which Tart would only talk to Kra in inaudible mumbles. Then he would clean his forecasting equipment and review his report for the next day. After that he would send his report through the pipe for it to be distributed to the public by eight o'clock. Then, he would toil at the forecast for the day after the next, only stopping to take his clumsy meals. Two hours after sundown, Tart would finish his work and spend the rest of the evening reading or thinking about the quiet universe in which he lived. He rarely had visitors, but the most frequent was an old lady who lived by the wharfs. As she deteriorated with age she became more convinced that she was his aunt and betook herself to making sure he never ran out of goat cheese and rough rye bread. That was it. His days were well-forecast, just like the weather.

Today, the reason that he woke up every day had ceased to exist. For years the people of Linett had depended on his forecasts to help them plan festivals, fishing contests and seaside weddings. Now they would depend on a lifeless machine and he...would be erased from life completely.

Going over and talking to Cypress Korkul, whoever she was, was completely out of the question. Simply not a good idea. It was ridiculous. What would he gain by talking to her? He was not going to grovel for his job back. Besides, a celebrated inventor would not indulge his backwardness.

He would go to her first thing in the morning.

CHAPTER
FOUR

TART PREPARED A SPEECH between the folds of his blanket and the caves in his pillow. As the night wore on, so did his words. By morning, he had decided an honest and direct approach was best.

But the scenario was astonishingly different from what he had imagined. He pictured a circus clown making a mocking parody of his life. He resented that clown very much.

Behind the chief's desk, which was now impeccably tidy, sat the very much disliked Cypress Korkul, a short skinny little girl whose head barely rose above the edge of the desk. Her dull black hair hung in two meticulous braids against her shoulders. Her little hands were primly intertwined on the desk as though she had owned it for the past ten years. On her small olive-shaped face she wore a bored and very un-childlike expression. Her skin was very white. Her brows were very dark, thick, and fully curved. She wore round spectacles with brass rims. She did not look very endearing.

The speech that he had prepared was permanently erased from his mind. The thought of talking to a woman had put him in so vulnerable a state that he had lost his sleep. Now, before him, he was confronted with an entirely unexplored version of the female sex, at least as far as *he* was concerned—a girl. How was he supposed to confront a little girl? Little boys were manageable. He had been a little boy once. Girls were little beasts!

"*You* invented the weather-thingy?"

"The weathernose, yes," she answered. Her voice was tiny and taut. It reminded him of the minute creaking of sails.

"B-but..." he stammered. A long pause followed. "*Whyyy?*"

Cypress did not answer. She only raised her brows.

"Is everybody in the department all right with this?" he asked.

"Of course, they are. Why wouldn't they be?"

"Well, I'M not!"

He put his hands on his waist.

"I fail to see what's irritating you," she said.

"YOU, young lady, have lost me my job!"

A small smile broke into her face to reveal a flash of straight white teeth. "*You're* Tart, I presume."

"What in the world do you think you're doing, meddling where *grown-ups* work?"

At this, Cypress laughed. She laughed so hard and the sound of it was the only childish thing about her. "Grown-ups!" she exclaimed, chuckling, "That's amusing. You grown-ups don't know a thing about most things."

Who *was* this girl?

"Mr. Clockquirk said I would have some trouble with you," she continued. "He said you wouldn't be too happy."

There was the clown again, mocking. She and Mr. Clockquirk were friends, it seemed.

"Is this your idea of a joke? Is this *someone's* idea of a joke?"

The door opened and Katcha, the old janitor, hobbled in

with a fresh copy of the *Oracle*, the town newspaper. As Katcha strove to reach the desk, Tart caught a glimpse of Cypress's gloating face on the front page.

"Cypress, dear!" Katcha said, "There's a crowd outside asking for you."

"What do they want?"

"Journalists," he said. "They want to know if there will be smaller weathernoses, for home use, you know."

"What? No! Tell them not yet!"

"Yes, my dove."

"Go tell them that! And I'm *not* a dove!"

Katcha put the newspaper on the desk and pushed it toward her. The man grinned and looked like he wanted to pet her dark head. He seemed to fail in seeing how un-adorable she was.

Tart glowered at him when he caught his eye. Katcha shrank into his frail skin and hobbled out more quickly than he had come in.

"You didn't like the idea of little weathernoses all over town, did you?" Tart said.

"I'm afraid there's nothing I can do for you today, Tart. I hope you'll be on your way."

"You're afraid you will be sacked someday," Tart said, walking toward the desk. "You want to make sure you have at least one use around here. You're the only one who can work the thing, aren't you?"

She gave him a sweet smile. "Tart, I'm smarter than *you* at least."

"I want to see this invention!"

"I haven't allowed anyone near the weathernose and I don't intend to."

"Why?"

"Because you're all too old to understand it. *You* couldn't predict the storm the old-fashioned way, and you have your shirt buttoned up wrong!"

His shirt *was* buttoned up the wrong way.

"How did you know about my forecast?" he asked.

"You left it here yesterday. I had a laugh over a bowl of chips!"

"Where's the rest of the staff?" came his livid whisper.

"Why?"

"I need to speak with them."

Her smile turned into a wicked grin.

"What are you going to do? Overthrow me?"

"When exactly in—*how old are you*?"

"Ten."

"When exactly in ten years did you forget that you are a child?"

"Mr. Clockquirk hired me because I'm smart."

"Wrong!" he shouted. "He hired you because *he* is stupid!"

CHAPTER
FIVE

O N HIS WAY OUT, he stopped every two seconds to shake someone's hand and to hear condolences.

"So sorry, Tart! It was bad for you wasn't it? You can't deny the girl has spunk, though! She's whipped our budget into shape! Some left over for redecorating too!"

That explained the rabbit.

"Tart! O-o-oh! You're not the weatherman anymore! Doesn't mean we can't see you popping in here, though, does it? Leave that godforsaken island every once in a while! Get some fresh air!"

The air did not get fresher than it did on his island.

"Don't take it too hard, Tart! Things change…"

Things did change. That was the flow of life, which Tart was not ignorant of. He had lost his parents at thirteen. That was a change. He moved from the city. Another change. All manner of things changed, like the smooth plains of his skin wearing themselves into tiresome cracks and gorges, the feel of his knees whenever he bent them to climb a ladder. The weather changed, as often as did the seawater from hollow, to wave, to froth.

He knew that acceptance was the doctrine of the wise. He

always preached that to himself as he looked at the sameness of his beach, he, the emperor, the priest of his lone island, and when he did, he felt very wise indeed. Change was good.

But not when it was imposed on him by a self-satisfied child who could use some lessons in humility.

Tart found himself roaming aimlessly in the city. He never noticed them before, but posters about the upcoming Innovation Festival were everywhere. *This is what happens when you let people innovate! Weathernoses! We should all stop innovating and leave the world to its dumb pace,* he thought.

He sat on a meandering wall by the coast for long moments, seeking a thought to console him as his eyes grazed the horizon. The sun was a bountiful mistress today. Fishing boats dotted the aquamarine bay. Farther off, the image of a lazy draconian ship wavered, pinned tightly in place by the sea and the sky. He might as well have been that distant gauzy ship, knowing no harbor and possessing no sea; there was no place for him anywhere now.

Sol. The thought brought everything that played in his mind to a halt. The very image of Sol was what got Tart off the sorry wall and had him marching, at last, in a specific direction: Sol's bookshop.

Sol was one of the few people—perhaps the only one—who had mastered the fine craft of saying exactly the right things. The thought of the old man peering at him through his round spectacles was soothing, like chamomile tea.

The bookshop had the misfortune of being located in the heart of city clutter. It was barricaded by the pandemonium of traffic, the yowling of dogs, and Linettans conversing, as though in a contest of volume and musicality. A small plot of grass and comely flowers they called a garden was on one side of the bookshop. On the other, a mile of cramped houses stretched, knit tightly together so as not to let any air in.

Tart skipped up the couple of steps to the door of the bookshop eager for...

The silence. As soon he closed the door behind him, there was only the gentle *ring ring* of the chimes and then the soothing sound of nothing else.

The bookshop was a landscape unto itself where hills and valleys were books that were too much alive, too often used to be neatly tucked into bookshelves. There were bookshelves. Oh yes! Many of them! Too many in fact to seem credible in such a tight space. They rambled on to the back where a velvety shadow slept: Sol only allowed the perusal of the books there under his supervision. A single skylight offered the gift of a watery sun ray that illuminated shivering motes of dust. It was just enough light to make ink pounce off a page without overheating your head as you lingered in it. This was because over the years Sol had, in pockets of absentmindedness, often forgotten to clean the skylight so that it collected a lovely layer of pearlescent grime that diffused the direct sunlight above.

Tart wound his way between the piles. Instantly, he felt a buzz, a thrill, a lovelorn sensation. He had not been much of a reader himself but there was something about the bookshop, the air of reverence and adventure combined that made him feel as though he had entered a storeroom of just about any thought in the world. The sacredness of human thoughts and the possibilities they suggested, nay promised, always gave him the odd feeling that he was being offered a privilege he never earned and ought therefore to respect.

He prowled, taking care not to move a thing from its place. Sol was nowhere to be seen so he sat down directly underneath the beam from the skylight. The chair made a good attempt to make him drowsy but he refused the invitation. He began to read a silly thing about fishing bait because, frankly, it stopped him from thinking about Cypress Korkul—at least until Sol appeared.

"Ahem!"

Tart glanced up and around. "Sol?"

Sol, apparently, had been hiding behind a pile of books on the counter all along, reading in a chair. His voice came from that cavern in the corner where books bade farewell to the shop, more commonly known as the cash register.

"You know I'm always here," Sol said.

"When will you ever stop hiding behind the counter?"

"When will you start looking for me here?"

Tart stalked over to the counter, hands in his pockets. He peered over the books and sure enough there was Sol, bowing his bald head as though in prayer over a large impossible tome.

Sol smiled up at Tart. His grey eyes twinkled where they caught the light behind his brass-rimmed spectacles. He got up, arms wide for a brotherly embrace.

"Tart!" Sol said with a glance that travelled vertically over Tart. "My dear friend! I'm never quite used to how *odd* you are!"

"How odd *I* am? What do you call this?" Tart protested, indicating the labyrinthine bookshop.

"Prosperity!"

Sol maneuvered his slightly stout figure between the chair and the counter. He rubbed the residue of dust on his hands onto the apron that hugged his middle. After he set down a tower of books on the floor, another chair appeared that Tart had not noticed. On the seat lay today's newspaper, the front page dominated by a picture of the weathernose with a bold headline: THE WEATHERNOSE, A PRODIGIOUS INVENTION.

The image of the weathernose, a stout little machine with pipes shooting up its back and too many dials to keep track of, seared into his mind. He stared at the hateful thing as a way of getting back at it. It looked oddly like his grandfather's coffee-making machine. There was not much to be said about it in terms of looks but it did seem to operate through an intricate set of controls.

Tart came around the counter.

"Have a seat," Sol said.

Tart threw the newspaper aside, pretending not to have noticed the front page.

"How do you find anything in here?" he asked.

"I leave my books to play as they please," Sol said. "They always come when I need them."

"Do they go to your customers when they need them?"

Tart sat down and saw that behind yet another tower of books was the pristine profile of yet another person, reading a book that lay open on her little lap.

"Sari!" Tart cried. "You're here too!"

"I'm always here, Tart," Sari said.

The little doll peered at him from behind the books. Her cinnamon eyes were darker in this cool reading corner. Her short slender legs dangled off the stool where her stockinged feet rubbed themselves in tiny little motions. She returned to her book and instantly seemed to evanesce into the page, leaving her body behind.

Sari was Sol's granddaughter, a near repetition of him only heaps more endearing. She was an eight-year-old morsel who had already accumulated an abundance of knowledge that Tart thought scandalous to be found in the head of a child. Another prodigy. But this one knew humility, at least.

Tart had once come to visit Sol upon a balmy evening and had found a small dark figure slithering through the open dormer window on the spiraling roof of the bookshop. At first, he thought it was one of those urchins that splashed by the fishing boats and occasionally pulled off a fantastic array of pranks during the night. But when this inky shadow crept to a telescope, he recognized her as Sari. She had climbed on top of a box and was barely able to peer through the eyepiece. For a long time, she gently swiveled the lens left and right. Tart watched. She seemed even smaller set against the vast sequined heavens. He wondered if she was apt enough to find this or that planet, or even the nearer resident of the skies—the moon. He thought she was a picturesque sight and he admired her more than he remembered admiring anybody in a long time. Later, Sol explained that Sari was searching for life on the moon. Tart shrugged. It was a start at least.

Presently, Sol was observing him keenly.

"You seem out of sorts today!" he commented.

"I was well *inside* of sorts only yesterday morning!" Tart said.

"And then what happened?"

Tart sighed.

"I expected a visit from you," Sol said.

Tart was tired of people expecting his reaction.

"Why? You've heard?"

"A little bird told me that a certain Cypress Korkul has left you wanting for a job!"

Sol reached out and pinched Sari's cheek.

"You're the little bird?" Tart asked Sari. "How did you know?"

"Cypress is my friend," she said, then looked up with two round orbs of guilt.

"Since when? How can you be friends with that monster?"

"They met a week ago and swore to love and cherish science and knowledge together until death," Sol explained.

"So, your sweetness hasn't rubbed off on her yet?"

Sari blinked shyly and dove back into her book.

"You've met her?" Sol asked.

"I don't like her. Or the weathernose."

"I think it's a marvelous invention!"

"It's a machine! It has no senses, no mind or heart, no right to be!"

"It saves time."

"For what? Have you seen the scandalous amounts of dallying and loitering that plague this city?" Tart countered.

"It's a reassurance that our future is in the hands of the very young!"

"The very young need to be at school! I need my job, Sol!"

Sol observed him with a smile that slowly furnished the width of his face.

"I know you do."

"No one consulted me on this!"

"My dear friend, no one is consulted when new inventions are born, just as no one is consulted when children are born. The weathernose exists."

"She's just a little girl!"

"She's a genius!"

Tart's fury with Sol's lack of compassion made its way up to the thinly breaking surface.

"Tart!" Sol said. "It *is* unusual, but is there anything about this situation that is illogical or wrong?"

There wasn't. And that was the truth. Cypress had no manners but she seemed abnormally capable.

"I don't know what to do now. Everyone in the department seemed all right with it. Of course, *they* didn't lose their jobs."

"One man's worry is another's amusement."

"They dismissed me. Just like that. A new invention has cropped up in our department and we don't need you anymore, Tart. After all those years!"

He realized that in all the muck, there were feelings that were hurt. They had not thanked him for his past service.

"How very rude of them!" Sol said. "No other job they could offer you?"

"No. The department is well-stocked with people."

"Well Tart! A cup of tea is what you presently need. That always warms my thoughts. What about you?"

A noncommittal sound from Tart.

"You're always welcome to help me put all these books back where they belong. It would stop you complaining about it every time you come in and I could use an assistant," Sol said. Then, after a kind pause, "Until you get back on your feet, of course."

Another noncommittal sound from Tart.

The tea was brought. The tea was sipped. Tart had nothing more to say on the matter. He mentally trudged toward resignation. Until...

CHAPTER
SIX

RING! RING!

At first, he looked like a shepherd from a distant tundra as he stood in the glaring sunlight at the doorway. The gentle ring of the bell was too small a sound to announce the bulk of him. He stepped into the gloom. He had a brown fur hat on, which in this heat ought to have been confiscated. There was a large mustache that looked like two sardines were kissing right beneath his nose. His big tanned face was tinted with a flush. As big as he was, he looked just as benign as a pup.

"Sari, my girl!" he boomed.

Sari gave him a shy grin. "Hello, Mr. Korkul."

Sol leaned in and whispered, "This is Kriva Korkul, Cypress's father."

Tart put his teacup down. *What?*

It never occurred to him that that child had a parent. He simply supposed that she was brought into the world by a machine or a gadget such as a motor or a barometer. She might have been born inside the spinning corks of the big clock in the city square.

Kriva joined the humble group. "Water please, Sol," he panted. "It's been quite a walk from home. I wouldn't be surprised if there were fishes swimming in my armpits right now! Slow business today?"

"Like honey," Sol said.

"That's because you always disappear behind the counter."

Tart, who would normally have agreed, chose to scowl at him for the jibe.

"Kriva! This is Tart," Sol said. Tart would rather have remained anonymous.

"How'dje do!" Kriva said, shaking Tart's hand. He was the sort of person who squeezed the wrong part of the hand, at the base of the fingers. Tart decided he loathed the man.

"You were the weatherman, weren't you?" Kriva cried. "The only person I've heard of with a name like that! It's a marvelous world, isn't it? One day it's a chap like you telling us to put out our pots and pails to collect the rain and the next it's my daughter!"

Kriva took a sip from Tart's cup. "Water, Sol, please! This is too hot!"

He turned to Tart. "I don't mean to brag, of course. It can't have been pleasant for you, but isn't she something? Eh, Sol? Sari?"

Sol got up to fetch the water. Kriva put a big hammy hand on Sari's little head and ruffled her hair. He sat down and when his thirst was finally quenched, at the peril of everyone else, he chattered for a good twenty minutes about his daughter. He forgot no habit of hers, no tendency or quirk that he left unmentioned. A booklet about her might have been written in that quarter of an hour.

"She's never had a toy in her life," he said. "'Father, I would rather you give those inanimate things to those beasts in the sandbox,' she says. Why, my dear? Because they're too moronic!

That's what she called them! Moronic!"

Tart would dearly have loved to punctuate that statement with a decent belch.

"Kriva," Tart said, "where is the weathernose?"

"I don't know. It's in the workshop, I suppose. She's got a workshop, you know. I built it for her, once upon a summer when she was five."

"But you've never seen it?"

"I'm telling you I built it myself!"

"The weathernose, I mean."

"She loves a good thrill, Cypress. Mischievous! She gets that from me. I never tell anyone anything until they're positively scratching to know it!"

"I can see *that*," said Tart.

Kriva downed the last of the water with a great sigh of satisfaction. He stretched his arms back, almost knocking some books off the counter.

"So?" Tart insisted. "Have you?"

"Oh! No, only the designs and pictures in the newspapers, of course. Cypress is planning a big reveal at the science fair. Your own father, I said to her!"

"And what about the weather department?" Tart asked.

"That kook of a Clockquirk's seen it of course, inspected it, and he was overcome with an instant need to go on sabbatical! She's more than a match for me, he said! I warned him that Cypress does produce flops every now and then, but he assured me the thing was solid and truly effective."

Tart poured himself some more tea and gulped it down, burning himself. Kriva thumped him on the back. *I didn't choke,* Tart thought resentfully.

There was only one thing to know now.

"So, you built her a workshop?" Tart asked.

"Yes, it's really a shed—"

"Does she keep it locked?"

"Oh always, the little imp. One morning I—"

"Security? Booby traps?"

"I can't imagine anything worse than a mouse trap—"

"How does she get inside?"

"With a password. How else?"

Before Tart charged with the next question—

"I don't know it!" Kriva sputtered indignantly. "What's all this?"

Tart downed his tea and slammed the cup on the table. "Please excuse me!"

CHAPTER SEVEN

O nce he was outside, Tart had already formed a destructive plan. He meant to relish this plan in the sun, but he was interrupted by Sol coming out the door. Tart could feel Sol's chiding energy before he even turned around.

"Tart," Sol began.

"I don't want to hear it," Tart said.

"Tart, she's only a child."

"Exactly."

"Leave it be."

"I won't."

He marched off right into a noisy huddle of boys playing a ball game. For the first time in this city, the pandemonium did not bother him.

He walked to the other side of the island for the first tool on his sleuthing list: binoculars, which, oddly enough, he had never owned. Secondly, he went to buy new cylinders for his palm-sized phonograph.

It was not much of a plan really, just a simple, logical method to learn Cypress's password. He was sure someone must have done this before. It was not entirely unthinkable that someone had sent their crow to spy on a little girl with a small phonograph tied to its neck before. It must have been quite common.

Tart tried to sound nonchalant when he asked for directions to the Korkul residence so as not to seem suspicious—or, at least, that was his own guilty rationale. Armed with binoculars, a phonograph, and Kra, he found a small dilapidated shack just at the foot of the hill on which stood the Korkul residence. He could see the shed just a little way off from the house, connected by way of a curving path that must have been encouraged by a wheelbarrow. The shed was an austere rectangular structure with very high windows underneath a slanting roof of metal sheets. It might have served in the barracks once before it settled down to become a workshop. Despite what he had learned so far about Cypress's no-nonsense mentality, a part of him had still naively expected the workshop to look something like a cloying dollhouse. He wondered if she kept weapons in there.

At six o'clock, the sun cocooned itself in a warm dying light. The redolence of the earth rose in the moisture and subdued heat. Tart's mission proved harder than he'd thought, as missions have a way of doing. He could see the lights on in the house, but despite his vigil, binoculars at the ready, Cypress did not appear.

He decided to wait it out through the night. The wilderness around him was slightly less hospitable by the time night had fallen. The sounds of wild things he could not see were enough reason to remain huddled behind the broken wall of the shack. He listened to the far-off hum of the sea and was lulled into a strange state of stillness. It was very pleasant. Until he had to slap a mosquito off his knee. And then another. And then a host of others.

The night wore on. Kra spent too much time up in the trees with the other crows, a sign that he was getting bored.

"Any moment Kra," Tart hissed. But he dropped into pockets of sleep quite often. He woke up with a start every time thinking he'd missed Cypress going into the shed. When he looked, however, he saw that the light in the shed was still off.

Soon it was light again. He glimpsed the first thread of dawn between the trees, just above the dirt road that ran along the cliffside to his left.

"Well Kra, it's time to go, I suppose."

"Kra!" the bird replied.

"Come on, you! Get down here!"

"Kra!"

"What?"

He saw an inky silhouette crossing the silken sheet of nude sky, from the house to the shed.

"Go! Go!" he said. Kra flew off.

"Wait! Come back!" he beckoned. Kra flew back. He had forgotten to turn on the phonograph that dangled from Kra's neck.

"Now go! Quick!"

Kra darted above the treetops. Across the hump of the hill Cypress went, taking every turn and curve of the dirt road to the shed. She stopped at the door, just as Kra lighted on the ledge above her head.

Tart prayed that in the semi-darkness she would see neither the crow nor the spying device attached to it. His mouth turned dry as he watched Cypress's long excruciating pause at the door. Eventually, he saw her mouth move before she went inside. It took her only a moment to retrieve something before she made her way back into the house.

Kra flew back. Glad to be rid of it, he bowed his head so that the phonograph would slide off into Tart's waiting palms and flew up to a tree branch to grumble to the other crows.

Tart turned the switch and watched the fragile cylinder spin. He heard the whispers of the woods and the cries of the distant crows in distorted segments of sound until Cypress's voice croaked in unequivocal authority.

"*Go away, Tart.*"

He could have sworn he felt a chill upon the breeze just then. He lifted his binoculars and looked through them at each and every window in the house. How had she seen him? All of a sudden, as he moved the edge of the viewfinder to the left, she was staring right at him through a pair of her own binoculars.

A fire of shame coursed through him. He put down his binoculars. It was a very disconcerting thing to be caught in a guilty act by a little girl.

CHAPTER EIGHT

THAT NIGHT TART DREAMT that he had a schoolmistress who looked like Cypress, only she was not Cypress. He was made to stand against the wall for not knowing the answer to one plus one. The number for some reason turned into musical notes, and he kept thinking as he stood against the wall that it was a horrible song anyway.

He dreamt that he had a daughter whom he was forced to call Cypress against his fervent objections. Kriva Korkul was his midwife, and according to the integral laws of the dream, whatever name the midwife chose stayed. Kriva, of course, thought there was no name more divine and worthy of Tart's child. Everyone in the dream ignored the fact that Tart was giving birth. And it hurt like hellfire.

The nightmares went on until dawn and then, at last, he dropped into a sweaty sleep and did not wake up until noon.

Disgusted with himself for having wasted a morning, he punished himself with a cold shower. Then he lay flat on the beach and slept again, having realized that there really was no point in having a routine anymore. When he woke up, he cleaned his toes and decided, finally, that he had time to pick the dirt from underneath his nails. His hat needed mending and his sandals needed new soles because they were starting to wear out.

He thought this would be a good time in his life to start a journal. Since it was decided for him that his life was no longer of use, that he was to be pushed even further out beyond the margins than he already was, it was a good time to start recording his experience and thoughts, perhaps a little vengefully. He started by addressing the general public whom he had been of good service to—he reminded them of that very beautifully—and then addressed everyone in the weather department. He forgave those he had never gotten along with. With a self-indulgent gulp of tea, he began to record his memoirs since childhood. He did not make it past his first memory, which involved the open mouth of a shark, before getting very bored with his own voice on paper.

He decided it was silly for people to write their memoirs, self-important, ugly in fact since, he believed, it came from the illusion that anyone's life is special. His certainly was not. He was not special. So, there you had it. The memoir was thrown aside.

Tart went back to sleep. The thought of repeating this day made him gag and it was all he could do not to crawl in bed and bawl.

He was suddenly overtaken not with grief over the job he lost, but with shame over the sameness of his life. Why did he live alone? Because he liked it, he answered himself. Despite the answer, however, he felt a wraith-like loneliness push in past his skin and squeeze his lungs with a fist of iron. He had no one, except maybe for Sol whenever he looked up from reading a book. What if he, Tart, died today? Now? How many people would attend his funeral? He suddenly wished he could not do math.

This wasteful attitude toward the day continued well into the afternoon. His heart was not in it when he decided to fish, so he found himself in his workshop instead, rummaging in an old apple crate for family pictures that he had long abandoned. His last shred of self-control was snipped into feeble tendrils when he found a precious leather parcel that had been sitting awfully quiet for years under rags and old newspapers splattered with paint.

He pulled it out, feeling a gentle tingle in his hands: the recognition of a childhood friend. He lifted the worn buttery leather and found inside a world of dreams that floated but never landed anywhere. His aero-machines. Sketches fervently lacing the rough surfaces of pages and pages of parchment. Smudges blotted out some intricate lines, but the designs showed through still. He was at once in the body of a twelve-year-old who believed so easily that he could fly grandly one day. His fingers trailed over the sketches of hot air balloons, blimps, and other aviation contraptions that he had fantasized about over many breakfasts, long enough to get a scolding about his food getting cold. That was all before the grown-up realization that he had empty pockets that needed to be filled and a place in the world that needed to be secured. So, into the crate the parcel had gone and was left there, forgotten.

A great burst of sadness rose out of nowhere, mixed with the curious wonder that his twelve-year-old self felt whenever a sketch was done. *Have you forgotten?* Something asked him. Then, before he could stop it, his eyes were leaking droplets. Oh no! There was another one! And another! This really was the last straw. To be crying!

At suppertime, Tart was thankful for the letter when it arrived because it meant his self-pitying episode was over. Kra brought it in. He stashed it on the kitchen table, made a circle around the ceiling then flew out to his perch to meditate. Tart thought there was something reproachful about his manner. It was as if he knew the contents of the letter.

Tart read it in one quick glance. It was very short.

Dear Tart,

As I have had the pleasure of knowing you today, I have found your company refreshing (Tart snorted here) *and well worth the opportunity to further our acquaintance.*

You are welcome to join me for dinner tomorrow night, along with Sol and a few of my friends. I would have dearly loved to introduce you to my daughter who is a fantastic conversationalist, as I may have mentioned today—and she really is a stimulating little person with all the little facts in her little head lined up nicely enough to make any old scientist want to eat his beard. You and I certainly are no match for her! At any rate, Cypress will not be able to join us, but I am hoping Sol's company and mine will suffice!

Please join us at six o'clock in the evening for coffee. Dinner will be served at eight o'clock.

Yours cheerfully,
Kriva Korkul

Tart knew what he had to do.

CHAPTER NINE

H E DECIDED NOT TO go empty-handed to the Korkuls' place. He came with a melon that he handpicked from the melon patch in his backyard. He hoped it was not the sweetest in the patch.

The Korkuls' house was by the sea, perched on a sloping cliff covered with a tangle of greenery scaling the rocks. The house was made of wood, curvy in shape. The roof was covered neatly in palm shavings.

Tart wished he had a plan, but he did not. So, he arrived an hour before dinner at Kriva's doorstep well-dressed, with a melon under his arm and no idea how to break into Cypress's workshop. But the weathernose had to be destroyed tonight!

Kriva greeted him with an onslaught of his usual chatter to which Tart turned a deaf ear. He shook hands with everyone whose hand needed shaking. Sol, he was informed, was taking a look at Kriva's book collection and would be down shortly.

The company took turns awkwardly offering Tart the best seat and he politely offered it to someone else until he finally found himself sitting on the ottoman next to the shrub in the corner. And so, the dinner engagement began.

The home, Tart observed, was an ordinary one: that is to

say it was clean and organized. There was not a great deal of fluff or fancy trimmings. The feminine touch, which included doilies and such, came from the housekeeper but even her contributions were meager.

Tart listened to Kriva retell stories about Cypress for about half an hour before he interrupted.

"Kriva! May I ask you what you do for a living?"

Kriva turned to him, astonished that someone would actually poke a hole right through his punch line.

"I make wood cabinets."

"Oh! And where do you work?"

"Upstairs in my bedroom."

"You're not afraid of stepping on a nail in the middle of the night? Why don't you have a workshop?"

"Oh, I gave that to Cypress as soon as she was old enough to start inventing."

"I can't imagine it was the military shrine that it is now when you were working in it!"

"No, no! It was a ramshackle hovel back then; not fit for you to store a dishrag in. Have you seen it?"

"Yes! Just a wee peek as I came up the pathway. Would you mind if I went out and took a look at it? I'm interested in the austere architecture. I'm actually quite surprised that Cypress has the stomach for it!"

"She's an eccentric kid, I agree. But I'm afraid I cannot let you near it. Cypress gets cross with me when I merely go outside, so I call her for dinner through the door. I don't know if it's because she wants to pretend that she has no father to boss her around in the middle of her epiphanies or if she simply does not trust anyone within a few feet of her work. But it is out-of-bounds. That's what she keeps telling me and what she would tell you now. It looks pretty much the same on all sides so you're not missing anything. It's more like a fort made of tall metal sheets if you ask me! Adorable if you can overlook the rust!"

That was that. But Tart bided his time. The evening was long. He took a tour around the first floor when the conversation bored him and found a small library with books that his parents used to have about all sorts of outdated topics. It was a dry little library that was only there as a custom, Tart supposed, so he did not bother reading anything.

On his way out, he noticed a small portrait of Abin Fernas hung crookedly above a chair. This was his childhood idol, the man who conquered the skies, who promised he would fly and did. It was commonly known that Mr. Fernas was the tycoon of the aviation industry on the archipelago with the first prototype of an aero-contraption credited to his name and currently being tested on the Cobalt waters. Tart tried to discern whether this photograph was taken by Kriva himself or if it was only a print that some housekeeper had hung for adornment without any knowledge of its significance. He decided it was probably the latter.

He straightened the frame.

"Mr. Fernas," Tart said with a salute.

Dinner was served at eight o'clock exactly. On their way to the dining table Kriva boasted of the fact that Cypress was on the verge of making a clock that would lock all the doors at dinnertime except for the door to the dining room to teach everyone in the household to be at the table on time. The household consisted of Kriva, the grumpy cook, a maid who came to clean only three times a week and Cypress herself. Tart wondered which came first, Cypress's genius or Kriva's constant encouragement of her confidence.

There were more courses than Tart expected there to be and more kinds of potatoes served than ought to have been acceptable at any table. It was like there were two cooks competing for the guests' approval and, in the heat of their rivalry, they'd ended up making the same food. Tart ate his potatoes in silence while everyone exchanged funny stories about life and Cypress.

Dinner went on forever. This was how Tart would have described it if he had someone at home to talk to. Dessert was a sweet potato pie. Tart speared a bit from his piece of pie and put it in his mouth, vowing that he would not eat any kind of potato for a month.

When all the dishes had been exhausted, the company rested on armchairs and sofas for drinks. Soon after the glasses were filled to the brim, Tart noticed that Kriva's face had turned a telltale shade of red. He obviously could not hold his drink. The eyes were bloodshot. The voice rose a few uncomfortable decibels. Where it danced in the glass before, the drink now sloshed and left some nasty stains on the furniture.

Tart somehow cut through Kriva's drunken bellowing, partly because it was unsightly and partly because he saw an opportunity not to be missed.

He leaned forward and looked intensely at Kriva. Kriva obliged him and leaned forward too. His sour spoiled breath was not to be escaped.

"Do you know the password to Cypress's workshop?" Tart whispered.

"The password?" Kriva asked, blinking in confusion.

"Yes. The password that opens the door."

Kriva looked like he was recalling something from the back compartment in his mind.

"The door to the workshop," Tart repeated. "I should very much like to see the weathernose."

"Oh! The weathernose! Yes!"

Kriva giggled like a boy who caught himself farting.

"The weathernose!" he kept saying between breaths as he laughed himself silly.

"I want to get inside," Tart explained.

"Tart! My house is your house! Just open any door you like, my friend."

"But the workshop is—"

"The workshop? There's a password for the workshop!"

"*Yes! What is it?*"

"Oh, I can't remember! Something to do with a dessert!"

"What sort of dessert?"

"Oh, I don't know! Try raspberry mousse!"

Tart rolled his eyes at the ceiling. In the merriment throughout which Sol played the fiddle, Tart went out unnoticed.

Sneaking out was no big feat as the conversation picked up in the parlor almost instantly. Tart glided out and closed the door behind him before the maid could see.

He rounded the corner of the house, keeping clear of the windows, and all at once, at the foot of the hill, the workshop appeared like a ghostly pile of discarded metal that furnaces had no stomach for.

He walked to it and stared straight up at the windows close to the flat roof. So, this was what it looked like up close. It was no longer an intimidating military stronghold. In fact, he could see cracks where the metal was welded together. He peered through one of the cracks but could only see darkness inside.

He went around to the door of the workshop. There it was:

the sound recorder. There was a single button. He pressed it. It blinked red. And waited.

"Raspberry mousse," he said.

The red light flickered then turned off. Wrong. Tart pressed the button again.

"Chocolate cake."

It turned off again.

"Almond brittle! Sweet potato pie! Strawberry ice cream! Orange sherbet!"

The recording device did not have a sweet tooth.

When Tart had recorded every single dessert he knew, he gave up on getting through with a password.

He circled the workshop in search of options. The walls were too high to be climbed. The windows were far out of reach. They resembled very high eyebrows on a long face. There were no holes, no cracks, no flaws in the structure.

And then he saw it. The tree. It was stationed like a sentry at one of the corners, with a branch outstretched. If he climbed it, he could wriggle across the branch and perhaps push the window open with his foot and, maybe, make a suicidal crawl in through it. He decided it was worth it.

He climbed the tree in no way like an expert. He was thankful that no children were around to observe him scrape every inch of exposed skin as he clambered upward on terribly shaky footing.

When he was finally level with the branch, he came to realize what a ridiculous mission this was. But by now it was too late. The view of the ground was already making him dizzy and his body cried out that there was no way down—at least, he was not willing to suffer a horrific venture downwards in the dark, possibly sliding down the thick trunk and breaking his neck with a fall. His only option was the branch that extended toward the window of the workshop. It did not look as safe now as it had from the ground.

Nevertheless, he was forced to make an enormous decision to crawl across the branch. He thought if chameleons could do it, then so could he. In his mind, he believed he could achieve a perfect emulation if he pictured his arms to be a chameleon's arms and his legs to be a chameleon's legs, crawling thus deftly across. What happened in reality, however, was that as soon as his awkward and bendy arms and legs crawled a few inches across, his weight became too much for the branch. He slipped sideways and, to save himself from falling, held on to the branch with his hands. He swung with his feet in the air like a mat being aired.

In such moments of acute danger—and he was in acute danger—the preposterousness of the situation halted all reason. For Tart, at the moment, there really was only one available option and that was to inch across with his hands until he could push that window open and somehow stack his weight from the branch onto the windowsill. When he arrived at the tip of the branch, having pulled several muscles to get there, he came to a horrific realization. The tip of the branch could not bear his weight and the window was a couple of inches out of reach from his outstretched foot. He had calculated the distance incorrectly.

He heard a crack.

"*Heeeeelp!*"

CHAPTER TEN

I T IS HUMILIATING TO be caught red-handed, but to put yourself in a position where you are crying at the top of your lungs to be caught red-handed is beyond insufferable.

Tart bellowed until the entire party came running outside and stood below him, looking up at his precarious struggle against gravity. He felt like he was being exposed naked before society in its entirety. What a perfect idiot he was making of himself in this very moment.

Kriva was the most astonished. The scene was so shocking that he sobered up and began sputtering indignantly.

"Tart!" he bellowed. "What's the meaning of this?"

"Help me get down, Kriva. I beg you!"

"You sneaking two-faced son of a harlot! That's my daughter's privacy you're trespassing upon!"

Two fellows aided each other in climbing the tree but found it impossible to bring him down without splitting the branch asunder.

"Tell me the truth, Tart!" Kriva cried. "Did you come here to break into the workshop?"

Tart winced.

"Did you?" Kriva pressed.

"Yes."

"I knew it!"

Kriva turned to Sol. "I told you I knew it!"

He turned to Tart. "You used me to get the password, didn't you? *Didn't you?* From the day I first met you, I knew—"

"It was only yesterday!" Tart said uselessly.

"—but I told myself, Kriva, a fully-grown man—how old are you? How old are you, Tart?"

"Forty-three next Tuesday."

"That makes you an old man—"

"I'm not that old!"

"A spiteful old man! I had a feeling about it at the bookshop, but I told myself, Kriva, give the man a chance. He's just lost his job! But this!"

Tart could find no words because shame was too powerful a silencer.

"Preying on a little girl!" Kriva continued. "Look at him!"

They all looked.

The branch creaked loudly.

"Kriva! I need to get down!" Tart pleaded.

"You live alone. You spit on people's hospitality, like you've done tonight from the moment you rang the doorbell. Our food is not good enough for you—"

"It's just—the potatoes, Kriva! There are other vegetables, you know!"

"POTATOES EH? SHUT UP OR I'LL DRAG YOU DOWN TO THE KITCHEN AND STUFF AN ENTIRE SACK OF THEM DOWN YOUR THROAT! All the time you huff and puff like I've seen you do around everyone in the weather department. Yes, I have seen you before, you know! Stalking out of every situation that might cause you to have to open your mouth and say something nice to somebody! Not exactly a team player, are you?"

Not a team player indeed! He and Kra were a team!

"You want to know something, Tart?" Kriva continued. "You can't have the world run your way. You've got to bounce with the times! But someone like you? You're the sort of person people forget about. And, unfortunately for you, you're not getting any younger, because none of us standing here, except maybe for Sol because he's a charitable man, would come to your funeral!"

The pain of these words hit him in his exposed gut. It was like Kriva had been privy to his thoughts a few days ago. To have his *un*-popularity confirmed before the present company with his shirt riding up his abs and his tired hands about to give way at any second was not to be borne. In that moment, to test how far and ugly things could get, a band of photographers and journalists appeared around the house. Tart could hear snapshots being taken of him.

Kriva waved at one of his friends. "Go and shoo these goons away, quick! I won't have a scandal."

Then he turned to Tart. "Or perhaps a scandal is what you deserve!"

"I lost my job, Kriva. My life," Tart said brokenly. "I have nothing."

"Get down from there!" Kriva cried, no longer listening. "Someone fetch a ladder!"

"I have no one," Tart said to himself.

Craaack.

Tart fell and could remember little else after that.

CHAPTER ELEVEN

ASIDE FROM BODY ACHES and a severe concussion, Tart survived the fall. What kept him in bed was the torrent of gossip that circulated in town. Apparently, he was *deranged.*

Tart let out a series of groans a little too melodramatically because the only one he could get sympathy from was Kra.

"You're glad you weren't a part of this, aren't you?" Tart grumbled.

The mailman came that morning with the newspaper. Tart skipped the headlines. He flipped to the last page: *Linett Gossip.* A picture of Cypress and Kriva screamed at him from the bottom left corner.

LINETT'S WEATHERMAN COMMITS BURGLARY

No one escapes jealousy. Not even a forty-three-year-old weatherman whose job was snatched (Well at least they admitted it! Tart thought) *by ten-year-old Cypress Korkul. At 10:20 pm Tart Morning was found hanging from a branch inches away from an open window of Korkul's workshop, where she keeps the renowned weathernose—*

Tart threw the newspaper at the opposite wall where it landed on the floor like banana skins. It was time to get up and go hunting for a job. He only had one can of tuna left.

The weather department had no open posts. He would have liked to work in a warehouse, but the warehouses would not take him because of the article in the newspaper. They wanted no burglars on their payroll. He worked for a week as a sentry but was fired when he cocooned himself inside his kiosk and refused to open the window to speak to visitors. No government entities would take him for his reputedly deranged behavior. He tried the fisheries, the bakeries, and the shoemaker's tannery. The tailor, the candlestick maker, the plumber, and several gardeners also contributed to his now-nonexistent career. The clockmaker said his fingers were not fine enough. Lastly, he stood in front of Sol's bookshop, this time not as a friend but as a desperate vagrant.

Sol was not reading. The harpsichord in the nook by the window was sending dissonant jolts of music throughout the shop.

Tart watched as Sol referred to the tuning fork and then tuned the keys accordingly with the tuning hammer. He put down the hammer and played a short melody after the adjustment with a far-off smile directed absently at the wall. He did so several times, tuning, then playing. He seemed so at ease with life, with the afternoon, with where he was and what he was doing. He had everything and everyone he needed to be king of his own life in this very moment.

"Hello Sol," Tart said.

Sol twisted around on his bench. "Tart, I didn't hear you come in."

"You looked so sacred I couldn't disturb you."

Tart peeked behind the counter, and sure enough there appeared a small cinnamon head that was nodding along to the words of a book.

"Sari." He acknowledged her, but she gave him nothing in return. She simply turned the page.

"Sari has nothing to say to you, Tart," Sol said simply.

"Heavens! Why?"

Sari shut her book and walked out of earshot.

"That bad, eh?" Tart commented.

"She is Cypress's best friend," Sol said.

"And that means—"

"That means that with all the talk about you—"

"I understand," Tart admitted.

"Tart!"

"What?"

"Sit down!"

Tart sat on a stool opposite the bench.

"I cannot reprimand you," Sol said, "because it is not my place. But—"

He stopped to think with a pursed lip.

"—what in the name of Holstromm's dictionary [1] were you thinking?!"

"You don't need to worry about my behavior any longer, Sol."

"Why?"

"Because if I walk out of here empty-handed, then I will have no choice but to leave Linett."

---

[1] Holstromm's Dictionary is not really a dictionary. It is a guide to all that is good and flourishing throughout the ages, sort of like an almanac for the human race. Sol has only one copy and considers it to be the most revered book in his shop, such that he is hesitant to sell it and has the habit of hiding it behind shell-collecting books, which no one is really interested in.

"Leave! Why, surely it's not the article—"

"That and, well, it's become quite sparse I'm afraid in this part of the archipelago. No job, no living. And that's where you come in."

Sol turned from him and stared at the keys of the harpsichord.

"I had no idea it was so dire for you," he said.

"I want to organize your bookshop, Sol. For pay."

"I see."

Sol tried the trill of a melody on the higher end of the scale. Then he withdrew his hand as if the keys—or a thought in his mind—had scalded him.

"I cannot, I'm afraid."

"But you offered before! Don't tell me you think I'm deranged too!"

"It's not that. It's Sari."

He turned to glance at her. "She will not want you working here. Unless she forgives you."

He went back to tuning the harpsichord as though no disruption had occurred. Surely it was a bit much to indulge yet another child? But he knew what he had to do.

He approached the frail little girl, almost like she would fly away if he were not prudent. He sat on his haunches to reach her eye-level where she was sitting.

"Sari?"

"You don't need to sit like that," she said. "It's insulting."

Oh dear! He got up and leaned against a bookshelf.

"Are you enjoying your book?"

She continued to read.

"Clearly you are," he said. "How much time did it take you to find it?"

She looked up. "We like our bookshop just the way it is, thank you very much."

"That's because you haven't seen it any other way. Just as you haven't even tried to understand my position."

"I don't care."

"Going to make it difficult, eh?" he commented. "Well, what is it then? What will it take for you to forgive me?"

Sari looked up. "You need to apologize."

"Did I tell you how sorry I am—"

"To her."

"What? Never!"

"I can find any book around here, you know."

"I'll write her a letter," Tart negotiated.

"No. You must speak to her in person."

She went back to reading. Sol strolled over.

"Benefits, sick leave, and pension," he said. "Plus, you can use my motor car to get here from the dock. If you speak to Cypress."

Can the waves refuse to roll onto shore? He gave in.

"All right!"

"All right what?"

"I'll do it!"

Sari gave him a smile that would have melted chocolate.

CHAPTER
TWELVE

I T WAS HARD TO walk into the weather department without bumping into somebody that day. There were admirers from all over Linett and some distant islands who wanted to see the little girl genius. They all claimed that they came for "just a peek." By the looks of what they were carrying—books, photographs of Cypress, heirlooms and, most noticeably, pens—they were coming in for autographs.

Tart had to fight through a tight knot of people just to be able to see the door of Cypress's office.

"Excuse me!" he said as he pushed through. They protested. They whined. They pushed him back.

"I work here!" he cried.

"No, you don't!" a man said. "You're Tart Morning, aren't you? I saw you in the papers! You were fired!"

As the ring around him took notice of this sorry fact, Tart retreated to escape the hatred that was about to be launched at him. He made a long detour around the clusters of people until he inched his way through, very close to the door.

Between two heads, he could see Cypress at her desk, being served a whole array of treats: cookies, chocolate cake, a jar of peppermints, all pampering her obvious sweet tooth. There was a tall glass full of chocolate milk that was about to be knocked over by a roaming elbow. Cypress pulled the glass closer to her with a frown directed at the careless person. Then a plate appeared under her nose. On it, under the sunlight coming in through the window, shone the most glorious strawberry tart he had ever seen. It glistened wetly and almost burst into red-pigmented song.

"My favorite," he heard her say. Their eyes met.

If epiphanies could be heard, this one certainly would have shocked a hallway full of people into silence. Tart put his hands on his forehead to cease the rush of excitement. Strawberry tart. *Go away Tart. Something to do with desserts…*

Then he was on his ferry and very soon at home. He had to listen to it again. Every spongy cell in his body was shouting that he was on the verge of a discovery. It took him almost an hour to find the recording in all the clutter of the past few weeks; Kra was sleeping on it on his perch. He had no idea how the crow managed to get it up there or why, but he was thankful that it was still in good working order. He listened to it.

"Go away, Tart," Cypress's crisp voice commanded.

At first there seemed to be nothing there that was out of the ordinary. There was not the remotest clue to the discovery he was hoping to make. He replayed the recording about five times before he noticed the pause. The PAUSE.

Putting the pause into account, this was what the recording truly sounded like:

Go away—PAUSE—*Tart.*

Now that he thought about it, the way she said *Tart* sounded forlorn and separate from the first part of the sentence, like a disjointed limb. Tart. Tart! *Tart!* The word kept repeating in his mind, rising up the musical scale every time.

Kriva had given him a drunken nudge in the correct direction and he had not known it all this time. *Something to do with desserts.* Cypress had given him the final clue when she said that strawberry tart was her favorite dessert.

"Go away," Tart repeated. He caught a glint in Kra's beady eye. "That was to you, wasn't it?"

Kra had been perched close enough to record but he was waved away. Apparently, Cypress was not friends with crows. Which meant that…

Was it possible that the password to the workshop was in fact his own name?

Tart reflected that it was a lovely afternoon. Through the window, the clouds stirred themselves into cream, juicing the sun in the process and splashing it across the waves and it was a truly wonderful effect, that dotting of light across aquamarine pigment. It was surprising how much a small dose of hope changed how he looked at the sky and breathed the air. He set out to find the weathernose.

This time, Tart wasn't too careful about sneaking around the Korkuls' premises. Cypress was at work. Kriva was likely at work in his bedroom. There seemed to be no one around except the whispering waves below the cliffside and the mad seagulls answering back in shrieks.

He took the indirect route through the woods to conceal the burglary he was about to commit in open daylight. When he found himself around the back of the house, he stepped out of the greenery and into the clearing where the workshop was.

He encountered the door. It rose a few feet above him, a steel adversary speckled with rust and dents. A moment of preparation, a breath of anticipation. Tart pressed the red button. It lit up.

"Tart."

Click. A long dragging sound, like an applause, as the lock mechanically slid out. Then, it thundered into silence. "You may proceed," said a cool female voice from the recorder.

Tart tiptoed into the subtle gloom and the earthy smell of the shed's interior. He felt like he was entering the warm and humid belly of a laborious beaver. He saw...

He did not see the weathernose.

CHAPTER THIRTEEN

THE CEILING WAS HIGH. The shed concealed nothing. There was no unusual machinery. What did inhabit this secretive place were rows of tables neatly arranged with all sorts of weather forecasting gadgets that he was familiar with: barometers, heat indicators, frigidity loops, and storm collectors. The wind dial on the table to his right looked exactly like the one he had, made of the very same copper, in the exact same size. Its sensitive hair-thin needle looked very new and made a familiar buzzing sound, like a tiny mosquito. Having noticed it, his ears now tuned into the other sounds. The rattling of the rain reader and the air thickness meter. There was a pollen wand and a cloud-o-scope that could be stretched up through a flap in the ceiling. In a tray sitting on one of the work tables were moisture balls soaking up the moisture and looking ready to melt. There were bottles of chemicals, exactly like his own. There were other gadgets, all of which he used to operate the like of daily. It was nothing out of the ordinary.

Frames of sunlight dropped from the high windows like a spoken decree, and shielded from them, in a corner, there was a lone desk. He guessed that Kriva had built it especially for Cypress because it was short and stubby.

In fact, for all the secrecy, there was something very mundane about the place, a workaday quality that popped the balloon of excitement around Cypress and let all the air out in an instant. The only difference between this shed and his was that Cypress's stern aura was perceivable to any fresh skins that entered her workplace.

"Where is it?" Tart growled.

He looked around again with more intent and willed the damned thing to appear, but no weathernose or any hint of it did. For a minute, he had to put his greed for destruction in a box and think like a rational man.

Perhaps the weathernose was kept somewhere else. Perhaps this was to trick snooping people like him. Maybe this was Cypress's old working place before she invented the weathernose. What if she worked elsewhere now, where not even her father could find her?

He walked over to the desk and admired Cypress's landscaping skills. The piles of thin notebooks made a hedge on the varnished surface and the pencils were sharpened by a carpenter's standards and placed in a mathematically correct row.

In that corner where the desk was, Tart noticed something that both shocked him and filled him with a stream of cold jealousy. On the wall were sheets of parchment on which many familiar symbols were neatly written. He snatched some sheets from the wall in fury. They were baffling! They showed all types of weather predictions ranging between two months back and a few years to come. He let them fall to the ground like feathers and read the one that remained in his hand, which was written on with red ink. It showed the extreme weather circumstances of the two years that would follow...but it was unfinished.

Hurricane in 1332 –
15th day of the month

He glanced up at the details of the predictions at the top of the page.

Predictions concluded 26, 4, 1332 Hour 6:11 Morn.

This prediction was made this morning. He looked around the desk for more clues and his eyes fell on a little leather-bound book that looked like Cypress's journal. He sifted through the thing, date by date, until he found today's date.

Had no time to confirm year 1333 predictions today what with my new office responsibilities. Rain Reader needs new parts. I noticed some inaccuracy in its readings last night, which means I shall have to repeat the prediction process all over again once I buy the parts. Must pass by the shop today. I am very much ahead of things, however. Daily predictions have been ready for months. Handed them in yesterday. Impressed the office staff. Storm predictions of two years ahead will cause a sensation!

He looked up and found that the red ink bottle was not covered and the pen was still in it. Something drew his eyes downwards to the small footprints in the dirt that led to the door.

"Aaargh!" Tart cried and dropped the journal as though it were a creature with sharp pincers.

Then, the last bit of horror in this realization. His eyes fell on the little machine sitting in a dark corner that he had not noticed before. It was the weathernose he had seen on the front page of the newspaper at Sol's bookshop. He went to snatch it, hoping desperately that his nauseous realization was wrong...

He picked it up and turned it around. It was too small. Too insignificant. Too—

He understood why it reminded him of his grandfather's

coffee-making machine. It *was* a coffee-making machine with cardboard pipes and dials stuck to it with a great deal of glue, which the clever photography camouflaged in the picture on the front page of the newspaper.

A crimson seared up in his insides. The question *now* was not about the weathernose's location. It was about whether it really existed.

CHAPTER FOURTEEN

UNLIGHT SUDDENLY STREAMED IN from behind him. He felt the heat of it slapping his back.

"You found a way to get in, I see," said Cypress.

CHAPTER FIFTEEN

C *AUGHT*, SAID A SIREN in his head. But then…she was the one who should be in trouble.

He whirled around.

"Lock the door, Cypress," he ordered with a voice of constrained anger. "I don't think you want anyone to hear the conversation we are about to have."

She scowled at him. But she did as she was told.

"You've been a very naughty child," he started.

"Nothing gives you the right to break into and enter my workshop!" she cried.

"Now, now! You know you are more in the wrong than I am!"

Suddenly her eyes spat fire and she looked almost evil. "What do you *want*?" she growled.

"To prove that you are a fraud."

She glanced at the spot near his feet where her journal lay in the dust.

"Where is the weathernose, Cypress? The *real* weathernose!" he nearly yelled.

"It's not here," she replied, a slow smile showing the tips of her white teeth.

"*I can see that!*" he cried. "Where is it? Some other hiding place?"

"Yes."

He walked nearer to her. "Now, you look here! I may not be as abnormally smart as you are, you little pipsqueak, but I'm not stupid either! I knew there was something wrong with this whole thing from the start—"

"No, you didn't. You were only jealous."

"*Don't interrupt me you, impudent little cricket!*" he cried. "You're—you're minuscule! You're barely up to my hips! And without an inkling of manners! No wonder you lied to the whole world about your *invention*. There is no weathernose, is there Cypress? Now don't lie to me, young lady! I read your journal! I saw the coffee machine!"

"DON'T YOU SEE?" she shrieked back, a trick of the mind making her grow larger and larger. "I *AM* THE WEATHERNOSE!"

CHAPTER
SIXTEEN

T HEY STARED AT EACH other, both throwing darts of intense dislike.

"What are you so angry about? You don't deserve your job, anyway!" she spat. "I'm smarter and I can do it much faster."

If it were not for the raggedy bit of restraint left, he would have smacked her this time. "At least I took my job honestly. I proved myself worthy. I didn't proliferate a monstrous lie to the world about an invention that doesn't exist!"

It did not seem to have any effect on her.

"And how the hell did you convince Clockquirk?" he demanded, "He never asked to see it?"

"No. He really needed that vacation." She replied with a grin.

"So, what did you say to him? I'll take over for you and while I'm at it, why don't I destroy Tart's career?"

"Your career has always been over, Tart. Do you know how many mistakes I counted in your calculations over the past five years?"

"Don't tell me you did your calculus at the age of five!"

Why didn't he just throw himself off a cliff!

"Clockquirk saw them too," she continued, "But he didn't believe anyone would trust me with your job because I'm only ten."

"So, you both fabricated this whole thing?"

"You're an awful weatherman! Stinking awful! The storms are never as torrential as you say! The hurricanes never come! And the weather is always cooler than you tell us it will be so that people end up cancelling their picnics and staying home when it would have been nice outside! Do you know what people used to say? He's timely and dedicated and he must be a nice person!"

That hurt. And she knew it. "You can't do your math and now everyone knows you're *not* a nice person, thanks to your tree climbing fiasco!"

"Can't say much about you either, you little sneak!" he retorted. It was like holding on to a rope that was already unraveling. "You convinced an entire city and maybe some buggers in the countryside that you're a child genius."

"I am a child genius. I just didn't produce the weathernose yet."

He stooped down to her eye level. "Do you know what happens to children who lie, Cypress?"

"They get kidnapped by the evil Sea Witch?" she asked in a bored monotone.

"No. They get told on."

In that second, their thoughts matched. Before their eyes, the picture of the journal popped up, fiery and black. They pounced, a tall long-legged man against a light-footed girl. Cypress got there first.

"GIVE IT TO ME!" Tart bellowed.

"NO!" she screamed back.

He strove to wrench it out of her arms.

"*Give it to me, you little monster!*"

She screamed and kicked him as he tried harder to yank it out of her hold. Finally, it broke free from her steel-like grip, his strength being the true judge of the battle. "*Aha!*" he shouted in glee.

She kicked him in the shins. He howled in pain and lost his balance. She grabbed the journal and ran out.

There was nothing to do but chase her and he did, down the pathway, into the woods and out the other side.

"Cypress!" he yelled. "There's no point running away. I already know the truth! We could end this peacefully with you returning to the healthy business of being a normal child or I can—"

At this point he was really out of breath. She was getting away around the corner of the boathouse at the end of the road.

He found her standing at the end of a long pier. He wondered why she would run out there and why she seemed so calm, so dangerously triumphant. He ventured onto the pier.

"Cypress," he said gingerly. "What—"

Her arm stretched out to her side, holding the journal over the edge of the pier.

"If you come one step closer, I'll throw it into the water," she said. She smiled like a she-fox. "Someone has to feed the fish."

"Cypress, don't forget that I could go to your father and tell him everything."

"Do you know how many figurines of you my father has carved and smashed? I don't think he would believe anything you say."

"I know the password."

"I can change it in a second, Tart," she said, rolling her eyes.

Tart was not ready to believe that this was it. He was not ready to go home, once again a rabid hound defeated by a sour-looking kitten.

"I can't believe this," he said to himself.

"What?"

"I said I can't believe this."

"You can't believe what? That I outsmarted you again?"

"No. I'm disappointed in you."

From the look on her face, her analytical mind froze, and it must have been a strange sensation. She said nothing but her arm lowered to her side. Perhaps she didn't even notice.

"Why are you disappointed, Tart?" she asked impatiently.

"Because you're—you're—well, you're a fortress!" he said.

"A what?"

"A fortress!" he cried out. "A rather short one! But you're strong and incredibly smart."

He took a step forward. She listened.

"You know how to conduct yourself. You're leading an entire department of people who before you arrived were, I admit, entirely clueless. You baffled the scientific community with your mathematical powers. You predicted the weather very accurately, more accurately than, well, I did over the last twenty years. Sometimes when I look at you, I really do forget that you're just a little girl—I know you don't like to hear it. But then it hits me and I'm amazed that you did all that in just a matter of two weeks! Two weeks! It takes me two weeks to do my spring cleaning!"

He was close to her now.

"And why are you disappointed?" she asked.

"Well you see, there are people who, when given the chance

to hear from someone else all the good things that they've been able to do in such a short amount of time, well, it so happens that they tend to forget the important matter at hand in the light of so much genuine and honest praise."

"What are you talking about?"

"I'm talking about the art of flattery."

"Meaning?"

"Meaning—that—*I got you!*"

He snatched the notebook from her and this time ran off with his shins flapping forward, pretty much the way an ostrich would run if it were leading a race.

"Tart!" Cypress screamed then growled so deeply it was a wonder that she had such a rumbly machine in her small belly.

Victory tasted like cool melon juice straight from the jug.

CHAPTER SEVENTEEN

H E DID NOT GO to the weather department right away. He decided to bask in his triumph.

And bask he did until nightfall. He sat at his kitchen table staring at the notebook with absolutely no will to do anything about it. He realized after hours of desperately looking the other way when a certain truth stared him in the face that, deep down, he could not bring himself to do it. There was a nasty hunch that he ought to spare Cypress the humiliation of exposure. How he hated those uninvited hunches! They sat there like cabbages in the bottom of his stomach, not saying a word.

She's a lying brat! he protested.

Really Tart. Have some self-respect. She's a child.

I have proof this time.

She's better than you at weather forecasting.

Tart had nothing to say to the long thunderous finger that was now shaking itself at him. So, he went to bed.

In the morning, he had an idea. It was based entirely on a dream he had about a hot air balloon, which he flew under the supervision of his pet sea monster. The monster was secretly his own mother. He could tell by the way she sneezed, but he did not wish to reveal that he knew because she would then ask him if her wrinkles were showing. And they were.

At any rate, he carried this idea with him to the weather department. It was starting to get warm. A few degrees higher than the past two days. He could sense it, even though he hadn't made any predictions since the beginning of the Cypress situation.

He did not mind the noise and the crowds as he shuffled absentmindedly through the city toward headquarters. He was getting used to it. He did not even notice when someone bumped into him. He bumped into several people himself.

He braced himself for another battle with Cypress's impressive fan base, but there was no one decking the halls in the department today and a hush fell over the place. He could even hear the water dripping in a nearby toilet through a door that was ajar.

He went to Cypress's office and knocked. The voice that answered was not hers.

He pushed the door open. Behind the desk sat the vice chief, looking very impatient.

"Oh, it's you, Tart," he said, sounding exasperated. "I've been interrupted quite frequently this morning. What do you want?"

"Where's Cypress?"

The vice chief blinked. Then a short squat laugh escaped him. "At school of course. Where did you think she would be?"

"*School?*" he asked.

"Yes."

"Cypress goes to *school?*"

"Of course! Children should be in school, shouldn't they?"

"What about her work?"

"Cypress doesn't need to be in all the time. She goes to

school twice a week, which is enough for a child of her intelligence. It's just to appease the other kids of course—just for show. And she's put me in charge in her absence."

He tugged his lapels down just then and sounded very important. Tart would have dearly loved to point out that there was no one in the department today for him to boss around and that was why Cypress had put him in charge today in the first place.

"Where is this school?" he asked.

The school, as it turned out, was a simple assembly of stucco box-like buildings stuck together in all sizes. The roofs were made of shaggy piles of palm shavings. The only thing that gave it a look of elegance and dignity was the wrought iron fence that enclosed it. The grassy enclosure that was the children's playground was dappled with shade and fuzzy splotches of purple wild flowers.

Tart looked at his watch. It would strike twelve in five minutes. He remembered always having lunch at twelve when he was a boy in school and he saw no reason for the system to change. He only hoped he would be allowed to enter the premises, let alone speak to the students.

The children came out much later than he expected. It was at the strike of one that they poured out of the main doors all eager for the sunlight, the shade, and soggy lunches their mothers had packed for them.

He could not spot Cypress in the throng of carefree children. He leaned over the fence and beckoned to a tall girl with a sunburned face. "Do you know where Cypress Korkul is?"

"Oh, you mean Lemon-Face?" she said with great pleasure.

Another girl sidled by her at the invitation of open sport.

"It's Sour-Face!" she corrected.

"*No*, it's Lemon-Face! I came up with it!" the first girl retorted.

A boy joined them with a ball hanging between his wrist and his armpit.

"You mean the freak with braids!" he said.

"I mean Cypress Korkul!" Tart said impatiently. "Where is she?"

"You mean General Kork-Screw!" another boy said, bringing the entire playground with him.

"Now listen, all of you! Tell me where she is or I will march right into the headmistress's office and tell her what smart mouths you all have!"

"You mean the headmaster," someone said.

If the children had been made of wax they would have melted under his glare.

"She's over there," said the littlest one, pointing at the rocky ridge at the edge of the playground, below which was the sea.

Tart remembered how horrid it was to be called Weather-Snot in school because he was always lifting the tip of his nose and smelling rain. But he could not help thinking that General Kork-Screw was not such a bad nickname to have.

CHAPTER EIGHTEEN

H E WENT TO THE very back of the buildings where a narrow lane bumped into a bulk of dark boulders that sloped down to meet the beach.

On the highest boulder sat a small figure in a black dress, as dark as the boulder itself. Around her neck was a vivid red scarf. Her braids were twitching in the wind. Her back was hunched over her knees. She could not see him as she was looking down into the mumbling sea.

"Cypress!" Tart called.

She turned her face. She saw him, looked puzzled for a moment, then glared at him very decidedly. For the first time since he met her, Tart saw tears forming in her furious eyes.

At first, he did not know what to do. He hesitated to sit down as though with one big puff of anger she could blow him away into the sea. Finally, and very slowly, he took a seat on a rock that was close to her to be safe.

"Cypress…"

At last, he saw the child in her. Through her dripping tears he saw all that she had for so long stuffed underneath her "grown up" shell: innocence, vulnerability, confusion, and a certain freshness, which people at his age had long forgotten. She pouted just like any of the children in the school playground. She sniffled and crossed her arms.

"Those children," he said as way of starting an awkward conversation, "they showed me where you were. Do you like them?"

She shook her head.

"They're not very nice to you, are they?"

Again, she shook her head.

"Where are your friends then?"

She was quiet for some time until her tiny unsure voice declared, "I don't have any."

They looked at the sea, Cypress embarrassed and Tart not knowing what to say. He wanted, for some reason, to say that he would be her friend if, you know, she needed one—just in case—but absolutely forbade himself. This was business and there was finally a manner of defeat about her. He had to use it to his advantage if he wanted his job back.

"I always sit here," she said softly.

"Do you think up your next experiments here?"

She looked at him in wonder, as though he had just tapped her heart with a gentle wand. With her smile, a dimple appeared on her right cheek (Tart had a weakness for dimples).

"How did you know?" she asked him.

"I just...did. It's easier to think when there's no one chattering nearby and nothing interesting to look at but the sky and the sea infinitely. Right?"

She looked shyly away from him.

"Listen, Cypress—"

"You told them about the weathernose."

"No. Not yet anyway."

She raised her eyebrows. She hadn't seen that coming.

"Why? Are you looking for my permission? Just like you did when you broke into my workshop?" she snapped.

The tantrum was beginning to rise again. The short moment in which there was something akin to understanding between the two of them disappeared as though it never existed.

"You're a thief!" she said more loudly. "I don't care that you're a grown-up and I don't care if it's rude! You're a *thief thief thief!*"

"Cypress, I've decided to make a deal with you," he replied, ignoring her outcry.

"I don't make deals with people who *steal* my things!"

"It's either this deal, my girl, or I *do* tell everyone at the weather department about your pretty little act of fraud."

She had no retort handy.

"I'm giving you a chance to rectify your mistake on your own," Tart reassured her.

Cypress was wiping away her tears, refusing to give in or even to answer.

"What do you know about hot air balloons?" he asked, his voice flitting away with a sudden gust of wind.

"Hot air balloons?"

He could almost see a big question mark hanging over her head.

"Do you know how to make a hot air balloon?" he asked.

"With a manual, I think I could."

"Good. Would your father allow you to get on one alone?"

"My father allows me to do anything I like!"

Exactly, thought Tart, pitying the girl.

"Do you think you could fly one successfully?" he asked.

"For what?"

"To win a race."

Her eyes lit up and she looked like she'd begun to see the whole picture.

"Do you mean the race at the Innovation Festival?"

"Mmhmm!"

She clapped her hands like a delighted chimp.

"Now, while we may seem to be competing with everybody else," Tart explained, "you and I will be competing against each other. Balloon to balloon. If you win, you get your journal back, you keep your position at the office, and you find me a job in the department. If I win, you hand the journal over yourself to the vice chief, confess everything, and I get my old job back."

"But even if I lose and confess everything, they might still want *me* to be the weathergirl as I'm much faster at it than you are anyway!"

Tart rolled his eyes. Was the girl ever going to have any modesty?

"I realize that. Once you confess, you will also tell them that you will step down from your position because the pressure of the job is getting in the way of your schoolwork because— ahem—school is very important!"

Cypress grinned almost wickedly. "I'm going to *WIN*!"

Her hand shot forward. Tart shook it.

"Nice scarf," he said.

"Thanks. It was my mother's."

CHAPTER NINETEEN

SNIP AND SEW, WEAVE then polish. The basket was taking shape. It was big enough to fit five people, the burner, emergency supplies, a box of sandwiches and a teapot. He meant to enjoy the trip in the open blue.

Tart had forgotten what it felt like to have an insistent energy keeping him happily up all night working. The wall in his workshop was now covered with designs that he meant to try out someday, so thickly covered it was like he had papered the wall twice. He stopped every now and then with a sandwich in his mouth to draw a new idea that materialized out of the invisible pages of his mind, unbidden, very natural like his thoughts and his dreams. There was a treasure chest in there, he realized, and it was getting richer by the minute. It all started with his little ice cream stained book of aviation designs. He thanked the twelve-year-old who secretly never wanted to be a weather forecaster.

As for the envelope—the balloon—itself, he sewed yards and yards of material that he stole from everywhere: from an abandoned warehouse, an old lady's yard, a tarp that had been blown into a field by the edge of the woods somewhere on the outskirts of Linett. He went looking for the things that people neglected. He even used an old bed sheet of his that he dyed red. He "borrowed" three cans of varnish that were propped against the wall behind a shoe store. The ropes he found easily at one of the ports at dawn before the fishermen woke to make a catch. When Sol asked about the design of the balloon, Tart thought it would suffice to say that the aerodynamics were perfectly sound, but the design itself would be a surprise, a Cypress-baffling surprise. He gave the basket its final black coat of paint and began immediately to work on the varnish, which he slathered on thickly.

This was no ordinary hot air balloon. This was going to be a generous splash across the front page of the newspapers.

CHAPTER TWENTY

TODAY WAS THE 146TH annual Innovation Festival. There were so many novelties showcased on a train of booths set up alongside the extensive seashore: cooling systems for beds, twelve-wheeled bicycles, pancake flippers, mechanic knitters, mechanic pea shellers, mechanic pigment mixers, anything as long as it was mechanic, *mechanic*, *MECHANIC!* Many of the novelties were missing a crucial element in their prototype, but so many more graduated the attempt and actually became inventions. There were some that were attempts by the inventor only to appear interested in this mechanical movement, to be part of the times, so to speak. For example, there seemed to be quite a lot of "nose-picking" devices that did nothing more than stuff a couple of fingers inside the nostril and then retract, only pushing the snot deeper inside. Then there was the machine that did nothing at all. Nevertheless, all of them were welcome in the spirit of innovation.

Food was the second most alluring affair. There were chilled sweets, punches, fried bananas, exotic teas and coffees, roasting legs of lamb, grilled corn, skewers of seasoned shrimp, and little iced cakes.

Entertainers were asked to come. Storytellers, smoke dancers, egg jugglers, clock masters, and singing peddlers. It was all parents could do to keep their children from running all of them at once.

Once the tourists had cleaned out the food carts, they meandered cluelessly in the arena. Few of them had guides who took them directly to the Fantastic booth where the infamous animechanics were showcased—animals made of steel, copper, and corks that moved with the help of a crank and spring-loaded motion. This year, it was a mammoth, two stories high. It barely moved at all before needing to be cranked again. Nevertheless, there was a playground of squealing children underneath it, running and skidding along with its clunky feet.

When those lucky tourists who had a guide were done with the novelty train, they were shown to the pavilion. It was set up on a rocky hillock, overlooking the sea. It was taller than the palm trees and wide enough for throngs to go in and out of comfortably. This was where the prize-winning inventions were displayed. In the center of the pavilion, right in the sweet spot of light that came in from above, there was a large hump of something covered in a sheet. Beneath it, the plaque read, 'The Weathernose.' A prim little girl stood beside it in a navy-blue dress and trim little shoes. She had her braids set in perfect symmetry on either collarbone. Her glasses seemed a natural part of her face. She stood with her hands behind her back, ready to answer any questions and quite ready to be fawned over.

Tart stood watching the scene in disbelief. There was a real weathernose now.

"Well, well, well," he muttered.

He jostled a few people to get to her.

"Hello, Tart," she said.

He bent down to look her fiercely in the eyes.

"You remember the deal?" he growled.

"Yes. Clearly."

"Then what are you doing?"

"I'm raising the stakes," she said, staring at him just as fiercely, "because when I win, people will have seen the weathernose with their own eyes."

"How are you going to make it work, silly-bum?"

"And now for the unveiling of the long-awaited weathernose!" an announcer shouted through a metal cone.

"Excuse me," Cypress said, brushing Tart aside.

The audience was all there in one breath, waiting. Cypress raised her hands with a flourish and then brought them down, sweeping the sheet off just as easily as you take air into your lungs.

"The weathernose!" she said.

It was a mountainous assembly of parts that looked like a sandcastle made of steel, wood, and copper. It had barometers and dials circling the central compartment, which looked like a steam chamber. The weathernose was polished. The weathernose was sleek. It had pointed metal turrets that shot up toward the top of the pavilion, ready to pierce the sky. It gleamed. It gloated. It whirred and sputtered. It *looked* like a weathernose.

A great "ahhh" sounded from the heart of the crowd like it was one awestruck beast. The applause travelled like the rise of a thousand butterflies with wings that clapped.

Cypress bowed with a solemn look on her face that Tart found distasteful on a child for its immediate dishonesty—at least he saw it that way.

The applause continued for quite some time. People from

various corners of the pavilion gathered at the sound to see what the ruckus was about.

"Thank you! Thank you!" said Cypress cordially. "I am humbled. It's nothing more than a creaking tin-pot! Really, Mr. Pollop! There's no need to kiss my hand!"

She snatched her hand from the drooling Mr. Pollop.

"Who has a question about the weathernose?" she asked.

"Did you make it all by yourself?" a man with a runny nose asked.

"Of course."

"I mean, with no adult supervision?"

Cypress's eyes narrowed for the shadow of a moment.

"I made it entirely on my own."

"Where did you get the parts, sweetheart? Things lying around the house?" a woman with a baby asked.

Cypress took a deep breath. "No. The parts were acquired from excellent craftsmen across Linett. Others like the compressed hydrogen cylinders were shipped to me from a laboratory in Hollumd. Any other questions?"

"Give us a forecast!" said the woman.

"What?"

"Show us how it works!"

"I can't."

"Why not?"

"Now, now, Cypress!" Tart intervened.

"These machines are more fragile than premature babies!" Cypress protested.

"Don't exaggerate!" Tart hissed.

The woman with the baby stalked off in a huff. But the rest who were unoffended remained.

"Besides, it's against the festival rules," Cypress added.

"Just for a moment!" someone cried. "Please! Just for a teensy bit!"

"No!" Cypress barked. "We're not allowed to operate the machines!"

The organizer of the festival walked in just then and was immediately alerted to the hubbub.

"What's all this?" he demanded.

"We want to see how the weathernose works," someone informed him.

The man pulled his slacks up. "I don't see why not!"

"But it's against the rules!" Cypress protested.

"We can bend the rules for you, chocolate chip!" he said. "Give it a spin!"

Tart was unsure if Cypress blanched just then because she had been called "chocolate chip or because she was just about to expose herself before a fanatic audience that did not seem to want to breathe until the weathernose was turned on.

"All right," she said. "Ah…let's see…"

She turned around and put her white knuckles on the table. Tart saw her squeeze her eyes shut and swallow. She was visibly sweating. She was obviously trembling. She looked like a rabbit that was about to be dipped into a pot of boiling water.

He crouched down before Cypress could do anything and tied his shoelaces. He made sure to bump the table with his shoulder when he got up, hard enough to cause the weathernose to tip over. And it did. It crashed magnificently, sending a clutter of metallic sound rippling throughout the pavilion. Heads turned to the center where a fragile heap of metal and wood lay irreparable on the floor. The gasps were unanimous. All heads then turned to Tart.

This was the perfect moment for Kriva to appear.

"YOU! YOU'LL STOP AT NOTHING!" Kriva bellowed. He jostled a few people and faced Tart. "GET THE NEWSPAPERS IN HERE! I WANT THEM TO SEE THIS!"

"Kriva! It was an accident I assure you!" Tart explained.

"I thought that ordeal in the papers would have taught you to stay away from her!"

"Please leave the papers out of this!" Tart cried.

At this point Cypress cried.

Kriva, upon seeing this, turned his attention to her. Tart sensed, however, that it was not the attention she was hoping for.

"Don't cry, Cypress! You'll make a new one, a better one!" Kriva said to her firmly.

"I don't want my broken machine in the papers!" she whimpered. The organizer crouched in front of Cypress to comfort her.

"No papers, then, dear. I won't let them in till this mess is cleaned up," he reassured her.

But Cypress kept her eyes on her father.

"I suppose so," Kriva mumbled. Then he pointed at Tart. "THROW HIM OUT!"

Tart was thrown out and all he could remember before he was hustled out and his nose met the sand was the hissing of the crowd.

CHAPTER
TWENTY-ONE

"THANK YOU FOR DESTROYING the weathernose," Cypress said. In the commotion that the adults were making to pick up the shattered weathernose, she had slipped out. She helped him up.

"My pleasure," Tart said, brushing the sand off. "Those tears weren't real, were they?"

"Of course not. I never cry."

"I'm sure you don't. I've never seen you do it," he said sarcastically.

She gave him a wry smile.

By the time they had taken the stroll down the racing arena, news of Tart's episode had travelled and it was in the wake of this news that the organizer of the race banned him from entering. She was a heavy-set woman who looked like she belonged in the endless depths of a library. Tart recognized her as Marna Something-or-other.

"What? What is this? Elementary school?" Tart sputtered. "Now I'm the one being treated like a child?"

Cypress cleared her throat. "Ahem."

Marna turned to her. She had a bottom lip that dangled like a camel's.

"I'm Cypress Korkul," Cypress said.

Marna straightened her spectacles. "Then why aren't you at the pavilion picking up the pieces?"

Cypress gave her a bored look. "Because people are still busy worshipping them."

"Oh," the woman said. "Well?"

"Tart must be in the race," Cypress stated.

"I'm afraid I cannot allow him in." She shook her head, shaking her lips as well, and returned to her book of contestants.

"Why not?" Cypress asked.

"Orders. Because of his abominable behavior destroying a little girl's invention!" Marna said. She looked up in search of someone in the crowd.

"That's stupid," Cypress said.

"Where are the Pokk brothers?" Marna called out to the waiting queue. "Since their balloons are going to be hitched together, I want them on the far end." Then to Cypress, "I beg your pardon?"

"I said that's stupid. It was my invention and I forgive him."

Marna chuckled in a manner that did not suit Cypress at all because it turned into a high note that was too amused.

"Think you've got Linett 'round your little finger, don't you?" Marna mocked. "It doesn't matter if you forgive him or not. He violated one of the festival's paramount rules which is *not* to destroy the inventions!"

"It was an accident!" Cypress and Tart cried at once.

"You just made that rule up!" Tart said to Marna.

The woman looked up and surveyed them both from top to bottom. "I did. It's common sense," she said. Then—

"Messrs. Pokk!" she called out, wending her way through the balloon-hungry crowd.

"But wait!" Cypress protested.

"I can't help you!" the woman said, waving a hand.

Cypress and Tart noticed two children standing on chairs behind the organizer's table. Tart recognized them as the girl and boy he had spoken to at Cypress's school. They called out names to the crowd from a list through large megaphones that were bigger than their own heads.

"Fylo! Hupple! Huqsible! Limewik!"

The queue moved forward, pushing Cypress and Tart aside.

"Come with me!" Tart said. He pushed through the queue again and stood in line.

"Hey! Go to the end of the line!" a man growled.

"You go to the end of the line!" Tart retorted. "This is my daughter and she's been punching and poking through this queue, but no one had the decency to let her through."

The man turned around and grumbled to himself loudly enough for Tart to hear. Cypress smiled up at Tart. He grinned.

They reached the table again and faced the two runts with megaphones.

"It's you, Lemon-Face!" the girl said.

"Name?" the boy asked with a smirk.

"You know my name," Cypress said.

"Name?" he asked again, the smirk settling even deeper in the cushions below his eyes.

"Cypress Korkul!"

"Hmm," he muttered as he drove his pencil deliberately down the page, then down the next and down the one after that. "I don't see it here."

"What?" both Tart and Cypress sputtered.

"Oh wait!" the boy said. He found something on the first page that was apparently a name. He crossed it and wrote something over it. He showed it to them. There was Cypress's full name with a fresh scratch crossing through it. On top of her name was an offensive scrawl: *General Kork-Screw.*

"You little ball of snot!" Tart said. "Who left you in charge anyway! Give me that!"

The boy snatched the list away.

"What are you doing in line? Didn't they ban you from the competition?"

"Yes, they did," Tart said, "but they had no right to."

"Doesn't matter, does it?" the boy replied. Then, to Cypress, "I will let *him* in under one condition."

He waited for Cypress to ask him what the condition was but she did not indulge. A fierce eyebrow remained raised on her face until he spoke again.

"The condition is that you take this little bucket of paint and this handy little brush and write your rightful name on your balloon."

He slammed a small tin bucket of black paint with the handy brush swimming against the rim. "We'll number the balloons with it later but you can take it now and do as you're told."

"Absolutely not!" Tart cried. A familiar anger growled inside him. It was the anger of a certain humiliated child whose ears had turned a blistering shade of red after being called Weather-Snot. He reached out and grabbed the boy's ear.

"I know who your father is and I am going to march you straight to him right now if you don't stuff that clever mouth of yours with rags and behave like someone any decent kid would want to have over after school!"

"My father's dead."

"Your mother then!"

The smirk disappeared.

Tart let go. The boy straightened up and picked up the list as if nothing had happened.

"I'm sorry. I can't help you, then," he said. "I'm only following orders. Tart Morning does not enter the competition."

"All right!" Cypress said.

"What was that?" the boy asked, barely containing his smirk.

"I'll do it."

Before Tart could grab the boy's ear again, Cypress had her hand around the knot of his cravat and pulled him down to her eye level.

"Tart. I'll do it. This is your only chance before that woman comes back. Let him sneak you in."

"But—"

"I don't care about the name. It's only a name."

It was more than that. They both knew it, but he admired her all the same.

"Two tickets *please*," she said to the boy, grabbing the bucket of paint. "And *please* point out our spots."

She looked up at Tart. "You know I only want to win."

"Yes, I know."

CHAPTER TWENTY-TWO

THREE HOURS BEFORE SUNSET, if you had seen the beach from an altitude, you would have seen an expanse of land strewn with blobs of color woven through with ropes and wicker. The balloons were spread out, burners burning, and behind them, closer to the cliffside, the entirety of Linett waited with their binoculars poised.

Slowly the envelopes rose from the ground and took shape as hot life filled them. A festival of color it ought to have been called for the hundred or so balloons shot up, each with its singular palette of colors, each a bouquet sprouting in a garden at top speed.

Then a hobbling creature so weary in his old age, shivering in his woolen coat in high summer, came to the podium. This was Addler Addlin, the great-great-grandson of the founder of the Innovation Festival back in the day when inventions were rare. As a matter of tradition, only the descendants of the Addlins had the honor of giving the speech — croaking it more like, for in the case of this little man the voice was beginning to wane like a far-off crow. A voice amplifier was propped under his drooping nose. He began the opening speech. He kept nodding his head to look down at the speech written for him on a trembling sheaf of paper and his mouth travelled away from the voice amplifier so that the speech sounded something like this:

"Ladies and gent...oys and girls. It is now time...nnual balloon race. As you can see some...ave already come up! Beautiful work there! Now as you all know...nd this is a reminder for those of you who don't know...point of the race is not to reach the destination...the balloons' speed is dependent entirely on the wind. The winner...fly their balloon to the island across from us..."

Here, he stopped to squint at the island hovering on the horizon to his left.

"Where is it? I can't see it," he said, forgetting that the voice amplifier was under his nose. He clutched his spectacles looking until someone was kind enough to point it out.

"Oh yes! I see it. Er...fly their balloon to the island across from us and touch down...line of torches. The most accurate touchdown...is the winner. There will...ime limit. The judges will announce...undown, which is three hours from now. With the help...eathernose we have been able to safely...wind will be in your favor and will indeed fly...cross. Is that Bart waving?"

He stopped again to squint, thumb and forefinger touching the spectacles.

"Yes, that's Bart, isn't it? Someone tell him to stop...er...aving like a hyperactive anemone. Contenders in your baskets and let's begin to take off!"

He lowered the sheaf of paper and took a deep breath. Someone whispered in his ear and he listened with a crinkly frown.

"Yes, I skipped that bit," he said, still ignoring the fact that the amplifier was still under his nose. "I'm tired and I need my peppermint rub."

He gave the paper to the gentleman who was whispering to him and stepped down with the help of his nurse. The gentleman cleared his throat. "That was Addler Addlin, ladies and gentlemen! Those of you who wish to see the balloons touch down are free to travel to the island by means of the fleet of ferries we have stationed for you at the pier. There will also be ferries coasting that bit of sea right there in case of any accidents. With the balloons that is!"

No one saw Tart sneaking to the podium when Addler Addlin was croaking his way through his speech, but by the time he was wheeled away, Tart had seized the amplifier.

"I-I have something to say—to all of you! One moment please, I really need to say this. I won't be long. Over the past few weeks I've been…so wretched. I lost my job. I lost…who I am really. I let myself lose some of my integrity. Funny how things tumble that way! Anyway! So, I came up here to apologize to all of you for my behavior. I will miss being your weatherman. As a peace offering, I made a hot air balloon that is, er, slightly different from the rest and I dedicate it to Cypress Korkul, the little inventor we have all come to love."

Cypress was already in her basket. She looked at him from across the arena with her hand on the edge, puzzled. She looked at him warily.

Later, her balloon went up, and for such a heroine she did not please the crowd this time. There was no applause when her creation floated off the ground, a simple white bulb full of air. Cypress Korkul was no artist. As the bulb took its taut shape, a tentative scrawl spread across the fabric with the offending title: General Kork-Screw.

On the other hand, when Tart's balloon began to inflate he

heard several delighted gasps from behind him, where people had flocked.

His balloon began to attract an audience. Slowly, the head rounded out as the hot air rushed in. The unmistakable braids shot out like serpents. The nose, the eyes, and the thin red mouth took shape. The throat of the balloon right beneath the chin was painted red and molded into a crinkle, just like her trademark scarf. Below the balloon, the wicker basket was painted black and had the oddest shape for a hot air balloon. It was shaped like a body in a dress with neat little legs and feet in shiny shoes underneath. A little further off, Cypress turned her dainty chin around to look. She saw *herself.*

"You're an artist, Tart!" someone called.

His balloon came off the ground; Cypress's head was big in the very literal sense. It bobbed in glee to the applause that broke out. Whistles and cheers followed. Even Kriva stared in awe. Everyone admired Cypress Korkul—as a balloon. Tart bowed to the applause.

"What are you doing?" Cypress called out crossly.

"I'm raising the stakes! You've got to live up to all this worship, haven't you?"

Her balloon began to rise and so did his. Tart lowered his goggles over his eyes and tightened the strap of his cap underneath his chin. He threw out his sandbags and off he went after her.

CHAPTER
TWENTY-THREE

F ROM HIGH UP, THE sea was a glistening sheet of jelly. Tart heard nothing up here. The crowd looked like a swarm of black ants on a white strip of land. There was nothing around him but a hazy sky mellowing down for the evening. He hummed to assure himself that he hadn't gone deaf. Only the shifting position of the beach below proved that he was actually moving. The other balloons floated around him at a steady pace, bobbing delicately with an eager wind. At moments, it seemed like they were all a bunch of party balloons hung from the sky.

He remembered his first flight. It was his seventh birthday. He had watched his father deftly heating the balloon at the exact moment when they wished to ascend higher. It was like a game. He would guess as they dipped closer to land when the heating would start again, for how long, and how far up they would rise.

"Tart, my boy," his father had said. "Always remember that up here, the birds are superior. So, keep one eye on the ground and one eye on the burner!"

It was not until he saw the sea approaching fast beneath him that he yelped and reheated the balloon. As soon as he caught up with the rest of the ballooners, he laughed out loud. A paternal blow from the afterlife smacked him full in the face for failing to apply a simple piece of advice.

Cypress was leading him by approximately twenty meters. She looked very cool, with her hands behind her back, very much like a general. When she turned, however, Tart could see that her face was stony. Was she scared?

He gave her a friendly wave and received only a raised brow.

CHAPTER
TWENTY-FOUR

I T WAS A SLOW race. He wondered whether the island getting closer was only an illusion or if he was actually floating backwards toward the beach. He welcomed every rush of wind that glided over his head because it meant he was getting there. His optimism broke down and he soon realized how boring this was and wondered who the genius was that came up with the idea of racing a hot air balloon. After all, they were only meant to decorate a sparse sky.

A pansy-splattered balloon performed the first touchdown. Landing seemed like a possibility again. Soon after, an orange balloon reached the island and began to descend.

Tart looked around for his opponent. She was flying above him. Her face peered over the edge of the basket so that she so suddenly looked like the child that she really was. Perhaps it was her height or the slightly worried look on her face, but Tart was seized by sudden regret over having coaxed her into possible danger. He kept his eyes on her as she scanned the skies quietly. He kept his eyes on the balloon too. Who knew how safe her balloon was? He was sure she had made it on her own, but with what skill? Knowledge was not enough to build hot air balloons. He himself had watched his own father build them multiple times. He'd helped him fly them and land them. What had he gotten Cypress into? And she was underage! He had learned upon his arrival earlier this afternoon that the festival committee had only allowed her to participate in the race because she was…well…she was the prodigy Cypress Korkul.

He spotted something as he ruminated over all of this. At first it looked like a big snake was crawling along the inside of Cypress's balloon, which he could peer through from his position. The snake wiggled unpleasantly like it was about to fall off. Then it dawned on him that it was not a snake at all. It was getting bigger and longer.

"CYPRESS!" he bellowed.

She didn't hear him because the wind caught his voice in its tail.

"CYPRESS!" he bellowed again. "THERE'S A RIP!"

She turned to him, shaking her head and putting a hand to her ear.

"THERE'S A RIP!" he yelled more loudly. He pointed frantically to the thing that would undo everything. But it was too late. By the time she looked up the rip was gaping, feeding on her balloon ravenously. The balloon began to dip.

Finally, the bulb of hot air that was inside the balloon gave in to destruction and the balloon crumpled into a helpless heap, sending basket, burner, Cypress and all falling toward the sea.

"NO! NO!" Tart screamed.

To jump from this height would be fatal. He lowered the burner to descend. He cursed every painstaking inch as the balloon headed toward the sea.

"This has got to be the slowest landing in history!" he cried.

He looked for a spot of red, for a little black head, but saw nothing. Raw panic was wedged in his throat now, in his gut.

He sweated profusely. He scanned the surface of the water again in the generous hope that he had missed her, but all was still and clear in the blue below. Did she hit the rocks? Or worse, a reef? Perhaps she was caught between the coral, unconscious. Why did they not mention the coral in the opening speech? He could not shake away the image of coral arms penetrating Cypress's head and coming out the other side like antlers. The blood. The corpse. It was all his fault.

"CYPRESS!" he screamed.

The balloon would have taken too long to land so he remained poised to jump as soon as he was at a reasonable height. He threw himself into the water, dangerously close to the rocks. In a second, he tunneled headfirst through dark voluptuous depths and came out to the surface sputtering and shaking water from his hair.

"Cypress!" he screamed. There was no sign of her and the promised ferries were too far.

He swam around, above and below the surface. He dove deeper looking for anything that was colored red.

He came out weeping. "Cypress! Oh God!"

An eddy of water licked the rocks to his left. He saw a shoe floating not too far from the rock, receding, nudging the rock, and then floating away again. He swam to it and hoped to everything that he knew to be holy and good that the shoe belonged to her.

He swam around the jumble of rocks and all at once was consumed with the image of a small creature in red floating by the rocks with her head twisted and her face in a pained slumber.

"Cypress!"

He fought the current to reach her. He put her upright and held her.

"Darling! Open your eyes! Open your eyes!"

He checked her head for any sign of injury, her neck, her arms. He rubbed her face.

"Please! Oh, please!" he pleaded, rubbing harder.

She stirred.

"Don't ever call me darling," she muttered.

CHAPTER TWENTY-FIVE

THE WORLD WAS UPRIGHT again and very wet. They both sat shivering on the rocks waiting for the ferries to find them. When Cypress was settled, she took her goggles off and a feeble splash of seawater trickled down her waxen face. She threw them into the sea angrily and put her face between her knees. At first, Tart thought she was relieving her sore eyes from the salt. However, the softness in his human nature recognized brokenness. She was crying.

He never knew how to comfort with words. Whenever put in such awkward situations, he was always the person who offered a glass of water to the distressed person. So, he peeled off his jacket. "I don't know how warm this will make you," he said, putting it around her. "It's sopping like a fish!"

She lifted her face from the confinement of her knees. The tears were streaming down her cheeks and reddened nose.

"Why the tears? Did you hurt yourself?"

She shook her head. "Just bruised from the impact."

"You must have been frightened, then?" he guessed.

She shook it again.

"You hate sitting here with me?"

"*I couldn't do a simple thing like stitch a few patches of cloth together properly!"* she howled.

"Well…" Tart muttered. He fought the urge to put an arm around her shaking shoulder. "Well…" he said again. The struggle for words was painful. "Sometimes," he began, "when—we can do great things—we stop knowing how to do the smaller things."

She looked at him, sampling what he said, rolling it around, moving it to and fro. It seemed to align with her brand of logic.

"That makes sense," she said. "I wish it didn't."

She wiped her salty face and salty nose. "You know things that I don't after all."

"What!" he exclaimed. "Of course, I do. I know that the hummingbird is the only bird that can fly backwards. Did you know that?"

"No." Then quickly she added, "I'm not very interested in birds."

"*And* that there is another city called Linett on the other side of the archipelago. Did you know that?"

"Everybody knows that."

"Right. Well…did you know that it's not really a city? Just a town with a lot of pride?"

"No."

"Yes! They were asked to change the sign to *The Town of Linett* so that tourists wouldn't confuse the two, but the mayor refused. And keeps refusing to this day, and to this day tourists end up there. There's even a joke about it: 'A town is not a city and a city is not a town—"

"—unless it was Linett!'" she finished.

A moment of nearness so endearing to Tart was when she clawed the slippery rocks just to slide a few inches closer to him.

"But most importantly," he continued, "I know that

sometimes people are not as nice as they seem to be."

He put an arm around her frail shoulder. "And sometimes—they're much much nicer than we thought."

She shriveled up in bashfulness with her elbows between her knees.

"So, I guess you won fair and square," she said.

Tart had dreamed of gloating ever since he met her, but he was silent now. They watched the orangey bald head of the sun dipping down the horizon. The ferries were still oblivious to the sorry fact that two ballooners were shivering on the rocks.

Cypress started sniffling again.

"What now?" Tart asked. "I thought you were mechanically incapable of crying! Is your machinery leaking?"

She shook her head, laughing. He nudged her.

"Come on! Tell me what it is! We won't be on this rock for long and who can tell whether I'll have the mind to listen to you blubbering again."

"I wish…I wish…"

"You wish what?"

"I wish you were my father!"

That struck him in a place so deep he'd had no idea it existed within him. The need to be somebody's somebody.

"Heavens no! You don't want me for a father!"

"I don't feel bad when I can't do something around you!" she sobbed. "My father doesn't love me. He doesn't put me to bed or read me stories and he gets so angry when I can't do something."

She sniffled and took a gulp of air to continue. "He wants me to be smart all the time! He thinks of me as a genius and it's no use being something else. I *hate* being smart!"

She buried her head between her knees and what she said

next Tart could barely hear for it was muffled. "I want to be like the other children. I want to have friends."

"B-but...you're not like the other children, Cypress," he said and shrugged as he searched for words. "You...never will be. I think—the best thing you could do is learn to be like them sometimes and, well, be different from them at others."

"Besides," he continued, "I-I like you. Very much. Despite the differences we've had. And Sari likes you too, doesn't she?"

"She goes to a different school."

"You know, no matter what grown-ups always say, *school* isn't the most important thing in the world!"

She gave him a reluctant half-smile.

"Plus," he said, "I know another thing that you might not."

"What is that?"

"I am a hundred percent sure that your father loves you very much. I've heard him talk about you like no one ever had a daughter before. In fact, he went on and on and *on* about how *stupendous* you were the other day at dinner. I wanted to stuff him with all that sweet potato till he couldn't speak!"

CHAPTER TWENTY-SIX

T HE WINNER OF THE race was Jojo Keen. Mr. Alamander came in second, and Hammon Flippet in third. Tart and Cypress came in last. Some argued they did not come in at all.

They were found by the ferries, and upon arrival at the island they were given blankets and two steaming mugs of milk and honey. The celebrations were held at the bonfire by the beach. The entire congregation was moved from the mainland and with them came trays of leftover food. The musicians were lined up again by the shore, their fiddles on their knees and their feet dug in where the water licked the shore. The revelry began as dark fell on the champions.

Tart found himself surrounded by a crowd of admirers. He was not used to being so admired. It was as uncomfortable as a tribe slathering hot wet mud on his naked skin.

"Where did you get the design?" someone asked.

"It's Cypress Korkul, you idiot! All he had to do was look at her!" someone else answered, and so the conversation continued with people speaking for him in enthusiasm and him not contributing a single word.

Until one portly gentleman appeared wearing a posh-looking coat that had the symbol of a propeller stitched into it.

He clapped a thick hand on Tart's shoulder.

"And the material, Mr. Morning? What about the material?" the man asked.

"I used different materials really. Coated with a fire-proof varnish of my own creation."

"Fire-proof!" the man said with a regal nod. It gave Tart the sense that he had won a prestigious prize.

"Quite so," Tart said.

"Mr. Morning!" the man announced—he never said a thing but rather announced it. He grabbed Tart's hand for a vigorous shake. "I'm Abin Fernas!"

His childhood hero was in front of him, weathered and worldly, looking like he had drunk all the saltwater in the world and eaten the gut of every kind of animal. He was tall, rich and taut like premium tanned leather.

"Mr. Fernas!" Tart said breathlessly. It was no use trying not to sound star struck.

"Have you got any more designs?" Mr. Fernas asked.

Tart, in his wide skip over the moon, forgot what the word was. The word was yes.

"Yes!" he said more forcefully than he meant. "Yes! I do!"

"Well then! How about a drink and a long talk! Let these people have their nonsense. You and I will share the stuff of dreams! How many more designs have you got exactly?"

Many! Loads! He had papered his whole house with them! Tart was grabbed and he let himself be grabbed gladly.

Later, when the bonfire had stewed itself into embers and half of the dizzy crowd had left, a toast was raised to Tart: "To the man who saved Cypress Korkul!"

"The next aviator!" Fernas cried. "You were meant to fly, son."

Tart crept away from the jubilation to find a family of two that sat cozily in a nook. Cypress was still wrapped in her blanket next to her father.

"Thank you for saving her," Kriva said. "She's a very capable girl, my Cypress, but she slipped. Just a tad, didn't you, Cy? You'll do better next time! Knot your thread and pull your needle like any seamstress!"

Tart watched the forlorn little figure, hiding in layers of fluff. He was still ashamed of himself for putting Cypress in jeopardy. But he was enraged even more that her own father had allowed it. He let nothing slip, though.

"Mr. Korkul?" he began. "Your daughter is a wonderful girl and she would make someone a very good friend someday."

Cypress's ebony eyes shone on him for half a moment. He smiled at her. She blushed. So, they were friends, now.

She turned to her father, emboldened.

"Papa!" she said. "Will you tell me a story tonight before I go to bed?"

"Whatever for?"

She turned back into her mechanical self and with her usual raised eyebrow and butter knife voice she said, "Because I would like it very much."

CHAPTER
TWENTY-SEVEN

Dear Tart,

News has reached me about Cypress Korkul and the weathernose hoax. While I cannot come to the department to sort this whole mess out—back needs straightening, you know, and I'm experiencing the oddest heart palpitations—I apologize deeply for the confusion this has caused you. I would give you back your post but as we all know by now, Cypress is the more ideal candidate. She has however requested, as deputy head of department, that you be offered one of three job descriptions...

Here Tart stopped reading aloud to Sol.

"Pah!" he exclaimed and threw the letter onto the table between them and stretched back. He did not need that job at the weather department, whatever it was. He had discovered something richer than gold and more satisfying than all the whipped cream on top of all the strawberry tarts in the world. He had recovered that his undeniable passion for flying still existed, alive and ready. The fact was he had always loved making things that flew. But he had never admitted to himself just how much.

Tea with Sol was a small celebratory ceremony after having just mailed Abin Fernas three of his best designs for an upcoming prototype of a line of hot air balloons. He had designed it so that the balloon itself was wide rather than long so that it could carry a comfortable chamber that could fit 10 people. The prototype was to be called the Glassmodeon.

Sol sipped his tea with the look of a sage who knew but chose not to speak and could barely contain his mirth.

"What?" Tart ventured. "What? *Tell me!*"

"I knew about the weathernose from the beginning," Sol confessed.

"You manipulating calculating book-soaked old man! Why didn't you tell me?"

Sol put his teacup down, enjoying the way the round bottom of the cup fit nicely into the round ridge inside the saucer. He put a hand on his mouth and thought for a moment with his two blue orbs glowing in the sliver of sunlight coming in from the skylight.

"You helped a little girl find herself," he said. "And if there is not enough value in that, you found so much more yourself. How much is Abin Fernas paying you for your designs?"

Sol chuckled. He leaned back and crossed his frail ankles.

"You're a good man, Tart. You're a good man."

Later, Tart climbed onto the rooftop of his hut and stood facing the magnificence of sea, sky, and wind. He stretched his arms out, welcoming the wind, hoping faintly that he could fly.

"How do you do it, old boy?" he asked Kra.

The wind greeted him in sheets flapping through his shirt. He took it off, the better to feel it on his bare chest.

He saw his creations floating between the cascading clouds in the sky, all of them delectable figments of his own imagination: hot air balloons, propeller aircrafts, airships with sails flapping where the birds used to reign. Who knew that all those dull years of predicting the weather were only the uncourageous version of flying through it?

◇

ABOUT THE AUTHOR

Maram Taibah lives in Kingston, Ontario. She has been friends with Tart and Cypress since 2006. She's a novelist, screenwriter and filmmaker. Her work dwells mostly in the realm of fantasy – sometimes her life as well.

She has written and directed two short films *Munukeer* (2014) and *Don't Go Too Far* (2017).

Also by Maram Taibah:
The Road to Elephants

If you would like to reach out to Maram about your thoughts on this book – or to say hi – follow her on Instagram : @maram.taibah
Or twitter: @maramtaibah

Made in the USA
Monee, IL
18 December 2019